DAMNATION:

THE GOTHIC GAME

FRAZER LEE

The Carpathian Mountains, 1897.

An impassable storm forces a group of travellers to disembark from their steam train and take shelter in a remote castle for the night. Their enigmatic host invites them to take part in some after-dinner entertainment. But as they each explore the castle's rooms and passageways, they discover they have become part of a deadly game. Only one guest may leave in the morning and it is up to each of them to use their wits, and weapons, to survive the night.

For the others, **Damnation** awaits.

Edited by Kris Rees.

Line editing by Julie Lewthwaite.

Proofreading by Isla Cahusac.

This book is a work of fiction. The names, characters, places, and incidents have been used fictitiously and are not to be construed as real. Any resemblance to persons, living or dead, actual events, locale or organizations is entirely coincidental.

ISBN: 979-8-36067-115-2

DAMNATION:

THE GOTHIC GAME

FRAZER LEE

DEDICATED WITH LOVE

To my favourite playmates,
Arthur & Rowan.
Thank you for suffocating me with prunes
and then drowning me in the moat!

ACKNOWLEDGEMENTS

Respectful thanks to
Kris Rees & all at Blackletter Games for
making my nightmares come true.
And to the original Gothic Game creators
Robert Wynne Simmons & Nigel Andrews,
who got the dice rolling.

PROLOGUE

The vertiginous stone stairwell is treacherous and narrow. Scant candlelight turns each footfall into a leap of faith. Sticky blood and the foul dust and detritus of ages congeal upon her skin, the sour, metallic odour overpowering all her other senses in the cloying dark.

Then, a cool breeze taunts her with the promise of escape from somewhere deep. Her forearms prickle with gooseflesh. She almost loses her footing and her free hand brushes against stone. It is freezing cold to the touch, and slick with a layer of slime. The further she descends, the more it feels as though these hideous, slimy walls are closing in, over and around her.

Swallowing her whole.

But she must keep going. The monstrous beast that hunts her treads evil into every step. She hears his heavy footfalls and the metallic scraping of his murder weapon against stone. She can feel her pursuer gaining and imagines his hot breath at the nape of her neck. She gasps. The tightening of fear at her throat makes each breath more desperate than the last. The stairwell narrows further still, accentuating her panic. She slips on the next uneven step and loses her footing. Hot wax spills from the candle, burning her hand. She gasps in pain.

Now, only the nub of the candle remains. It sputters, and she glimpses a phantasmagoria of shadows on the walls and the ceiling. The acrid smell of burning hairs on the back of her hand mingles with the salt tang of blood. In the flickering orange light of the candle, she glimpses the horrifying silhouette of a writhing girl tied to a stake. Phantom screams pierce her eardrums from within. The scent of burning hair worsens. Even worse, the sickening aftertaste of burning flesh causes bile to rise to her throat. She hears the girl's screams intensify inside her skull as the image distorts, enveloping the stairwell in a nightmare conflagration of pain and death. The heat laps at her tender flesh, hungrily.

Still, she battles on down the stairs. The candle sputters once more, and then dies. She is plunged into darkness and she feels it closing around her like the maw of some colossal, nocturnal beast. She tries to scream, but no sound will come.

Strong hands grip her, wrenching the breath from her body. For a moment she is weightless, floating puppet-like at the whim of those unseen hands. Then, she is propelled up and backwards until her back slams painfully against unyielding stone. She smells his breath, foul with rot and ruin. One hand drops from her shoulder and before she can even gasp, it is at her throat. The inhuman grip crushes her windpipe. Her legs spasm like those of a convict at the end of the hangman's rope. Her feet dangle uselessly, her toes inches above the floor. The fingers of his other hand insinuate themselves into her hair, coiling her tresses tight. She feels the roots of her hair tearing away as the hand pulls her head violently forward. Her throat burns dry with the urge to scream, to implore, to plead for mercy. But the hand silences her with its vice-like grip. Her world spins black and darker still as she feels her head slam against the wall, over and over, at impossible speed and with ferocious force – until blood runs hot down the back of her neck. His arm has become the piston of an insane machine designed to end her life. She feels the blood pooling beneath her dress at the small of her back. He loosens his grip and she feels herself sliding down the wall. Her legs buckle beneath her.

A broken doll in a pool of her own lifeblood – she will lie forgotten in that dark stairwell.

As the last trickle of blood leaves her body, she sees a light. If only her legs would move, she could crawl toward it! But in a moment the light is gone and there is only darkness, despair—

And damnation.

CHAPTER ONE

Mara jolted awake at the shrill sound of the whistle. She sat bolt upright, panting, and coughed the phantom of her nightmare away.

What an altogether horrid dream!

Placing her small hand at her throat, she half-expected to find it swollen and sore from the monster's grip.

Nothing.

Instinct then found her hand at the back of her head.

No blood. Just the after-effects of her disturbing nightmare. Reaching for the handrail beside her bed in the sleeper carriage, she steadied herself against the movement of the train and calmed her breathing.

She then used her free hand to disentangle her legs from her sheets, which were in some disarray. The small of her back felt cold, and she realised with shame that her nightdress was drenched with perspiration.

She arose and walked over to the wall-mounted gas lamp. It flickered, conjuring unwelcome memories of the candle and the crumbling stair from her dream. She reached up to the little brass wheel and dispelled her night terrors with a turn of the valve. Her cabin now fully illuminated, Mara crossed to the nightstand and poured water from a jug into a goblet. Her throat was dry and she did not cease drinking until she had drained the vessel. Composure returning with each passing second, she placed a hand to her breast and willed her heart to settle into something of a regular rhythm. Soon enough, her pulse returned to normal. The fire and blood of her nightmares had receded, leaving her to the order of the day.

Tucking a loose strand of hair behind her ear, she turned to survey the dress she had hung on the rail above her valise. She took the jug and poured the remainder of the water into the enamel bowl set into an alcove in the wall. Above it, a mirror revealed her reflection. The leading was beginning to show around the edges of the looking glass, casting a vignette around her reflected face. This only served to increase her focus. The hazel eyes looking back at her looked sharper now that she had fully emerged from her slumber, but her nightmares had left their dark, half-moon shadows beneath them. She gazed instead upon her olive skin, which had lost none of its lustre despite her travels. She blinked, her lashes like petals reaching for sunlight, coming back to life. Arching her spine (as a cat might, in readiness for the hunt), she licked her lips and felt hunger stirring in her belly. Taking a silk scarf from the back of the chair beside the sink, she tied back her hair and set about readying herself for breakfast.

***

The steam train thundered on, the track beneath its relentless metal wheels defying the tightrope ledge of a mountain range. If one were able to view it from above, from the vantage point of some carrion bird perhaps, the sleepers would describe the backbone of an enormous dragon. Legend spoke of such a beast, sleeping beneath these Carpathian peaks and dreaming of an Empire long forgotten.

The whistle emulated the cry of that legendary scaly beast, and the engine roared ever louder as it braved the mouth of an impenetrably black tunnel. A single lamp burned at the front of the engine, a blazing, lidless eye. Shadows danced on the tunnel walls as the carriages spilled their light through window blinds and onto the rough-hewn rock.

Thousands had died carving this tunnel through the mountain, their blood long since subsumed by stone. Men who came to the Carpathians – most as captives of war, some by some other cruel twist of fate – invariably perished with pickaxes in their hands. Each chink in the rock face served as an epitaph, and a warning not to tarry in the belly of this bestial land.

Mara could not but help hear the rattling of bones with each click and clack of the locomotive's wheels beneath the carriage. She grabbed onto the handrail, jostled by the movement of the train as it hurtled through the tunnel. Another sharp blare from the whistle, and the train emerged into the great outdoors once more. Mara felt relief to be out of the long dark of the tunnel. She paused for a moment, her breath taken away by the enormous vista before her. High mountains framed a turbulent sky, a river snaking beneath it into a vast lake. The surface of the lake reflected the heavens above, giving it the aspect of dark grey marble.

The hairs at the nape of her neck bristled, and she felt suddenly aware that someone was watching her. She glanced over her shoulder and saw an enormous figure in the walkway, moving toward her. The hulking giant seemed unperturbed by the rocking movement of the train, each massive step emulating that of a deep-sea diver. Mara turned and moved on, into the dining car.

The atmosphere inside was effulgent with the scents of cigarette smoke, candle wax, and the familiar beefy aroma of last night's consommé. One patron was already in mid-complaint about the breakfast menu. An ostentatiously dressed woman glanced at Mara, her sharp little eyes taking in every detail, apparently disapproving of her attire.

"Is there no one of good breeding present aboard this Godforsaken Hell-train?" she grumbled, as Mara passed by her table. "Savages!" the woman snapped at a bored-looking waiter, who then made the mistake of attempting to pour her tea without allowing it to brew first. "Heathens and savages, the bally lot of you," she went on, apparently addressing the entire dining car.

Mara was glad to put some distance between her and the unpleasant woman. A waiter pulled back her chair for her, and then made short work of placing a linen napkin over her lap. He presented the breakfast menu to her as though it were some arcane tome bearing hidden secrets. As soon as he had gone, Mara discarded the menu, dropping it into the empty place setting opposite. She already knew its meagre contents off by heart. Reaching into her clutch bag, she pulled out her tarot deck, wrapped in the same silk scarf she had used to tie her hair up earlier. She shuffled through the cards, her eyes surveying the car and its diners.

Mara pulled a card from the deck as she listened to the shrill voice of the irascible aristocrat. The unpleasant woman was castigating the staff again, this time for a piece of dirty cutlery. Mara looked at the woman and their eyes met; she enjoyed the growing look of outrage on the woman's face as she held her gaze. This was someone who looked down on others so much that they in turn looked to their feet. But not Mara. The flustered woman muttered something angrily, before looking away from Mara and trying to attract the attention of the harried waiter. Smiling to herself, Mara turned her attention to the card she had pulled from the tarot deck. She turned it over, revealing the *Two of Wands*. How apt, she thought, thinking of the aristocratic woman's sour expression.

Pulling another card, Mara held it in her hand as she glanced around the dining car. Tucked away in the shadows beneath an unlit wall lamp, she discerned a figure sitting stock-still. He, for the frame was doubtless that of a male, in contradiction to dining etiquette wore a black top hat which cast an impenetrable darkness over his countenance. He wore his frock coat, closely tailored in a similar dark hue, high at the collar to conceal the remainder of his face. Only his eyes were visible, glinting from the mysterious shadow that was his visage, and Mara found their cool, expressionless gaze disconcerting. She turned over the card. *The Hanged Man.* Interesting.

Another man sat at the table opposite, every inch an Englishman with his fine moustache and whiskers. He was effusive in his thanks; expressing gratitude for the waiter's every move when he poured the coffee, then the water, and even when he proffered the menu. Mara thought it must be utterly exhausting to be so overly polite all the while.

Yet, despite the fact that he was so buttoned-up, there was something frayed around the edges of this fellow. He appeared nervous and uncomfortable in his own body, a predicament that manifested itself in clumsiness. She watched with bemused interest as he managed to drop his butter knife and then, when he attempted to retrieve it from the dining car floor, knocked over his water glass. Mara considered how unpopular he must be at social functions. Anyone brave enough to accept the offer of a dance from this oaf would never escape with their toes intact. She extracted another card from her deck and set it down on the dining table: *The Fool.*

Just then, a shadow so sudden and so absolute fell over Mara that she thought the train must have entered another tunnel. Looking up, she saw the true source of the indomitable darkness. The huge man who had followed her along the walkways between carriages had arrived at the dining car. He was so tall, seven foot at least, that he had to stoop before entering lest the doorframe relieve him of his equally enormous hat. His headgear would have been more suited to the high plains of the Wild West than to a formal dining situation. The rest of the huge man's garb was also in the American style, with a dark waistcoat tightly buttoned over a flannel shirt. His broad shoulders carried a greatcoat that looked heavy enough to double as a storm shelter, and it was fashioned from heavily stitched hides of so many various shades and textures that when he moved the garment seemed as though it too were a living thing. Beneath his hat, the man's monstrous brow remained fixed in a frown as pronounced as the overhanging mountains below which they now travelled. He halted and surveyed the room with stark blue eyes which, contrary to the remainder of his sizeable presence, had a childlike aspect. It was to Mara as though he had plucked them from some young innocent's sockets to make them his own. He certainly looked capable of such dark deeds.

The huge man lumbered past her table, a cloud clearing the sun, and the warm glow of the gaslight returned to her. She watched him sit at a nearby table and heard the protestations of his chair as it creaked beneath his bulk. He swept aside his greatcoat as he sat down, and Mara saw a huge bowie knife secured at his hip within a sable sheath. The handle of the knife was immense, carved from a bone or antler large enough to match his supersized hands. He muttered instructions to the waiter under his breath and then waved him away. As he sipped his coffee, those bright eyes studied each occupant of the car in turn. It was as though he were cataloguing them, somehow. Perhaps he was.

Mara drew her next card and knew it to be *Death* before she had even flipped it over. Perhaps she and her cards had the measure of her fellow travellers too.

"Is this seat taken?"

It seemed to be a rhetorical question, as the man asking it of her had already seated himself before she could answer. He wore the Holy robes of a *strannik*, a pilgrim monk.

"Grigori Yefimovich Rasputin, at your service."

He proffered his right hand in greeting and Mara noticed how smooth his skin was. How long his nails were. She allowed him to kiss her hand, feeling the brush of his long beard against her flesh. She retrieved her hand from his unwelcome touch and placed it safely in her lap, on instinct.

"I see you are acquainted with the Art." He nodded at the tarot cards. "What is your name, dear child?"

She remained silent for the moment, feeling uneasy enough in his company not to want to give anything away to this dark man with his dark smile.

He grinned, revealing yellow teeth, and then chuckled amiably. "I fear I have intruded too much, forgive my manners, it has been a long journey and polite company has been difficult to come by." He glanced around the dining car at the rude aristocrat, the clumsy Englishman, the stoic American, and the shadowy stranger.

Mara had to concede that he had a point. She relented.

"It is my manners you must forgive," she said. "Please understand the predicament of a woman travelling … unaccompanied. My name is Mara."

His dark eyes widened. He repeated her name, emphasising both syllables as though they were delicious morsels. "Mara. Pleased to make your acquaintance." He clicked his fingers at the waiter. "Bring wine."

The waiter looked nonplussed. "If sir would like to select something from the *breakfast* menu—"

"I have selected *breakfast* wine. And you will bring it to me, now," Rasputin growled.

"For madam?" the waiter asked.

"Tea," Mara said, "black."

The waiter nodded and hurried away. Rasputin looked again at Mara's tarot cards. "Did they tell you anything interesting?"

"The cards? Oh, I merely dabble. Something to pass the time on a long journey when all the books have been read, and every inch of flora and fauna correctly identified."

"A challenge, then. To while away the remainder of the hour."

Mara raised an eyebrow. Rasputin's vertiginous cheekbones actually showed a blush of amusement as she did so.

"Read my fortune correctly."

She chuckled at his bravado. *Correctly*. If he knew the tarot as she suspected he did, he would know there was more of an art to it than a craft. The art of interpretation. Perhaps that was the challenge. To see behind the mystique he had so obviously and painstakingly built around himself. Behind that long, cascading beard there was the truth of a man. This was bait enough for Mara and she decided to take it.

"I shall draw one card only, and read your fortune as you say – correctly."

He nodded, and regarded her with quiet amusement as the waiter returned.

Mara closed her eyes, and pictured his face in her mind's eye. Hearing the waiter pour their drinks, she was reminded of Rasputin's long, flowing hair, parted at the centre where it had begun to thin. His angular, almost corvid features. The line of his mouth, framed by the dark flow of his ample beard. She focused on a place hidden behind all these surface details, a sanctuary concealed behind a fortress of flesh and bone. The very marrow of his being. His mortal soul.

The card had appeared in her hand without any sensation of having taken it from the deck. She opened her eyes. He reached across the table and gently gripped her wrist, then twisted it subtly until she turned the card over. *The Hierophant.* A flash of images invaded her mind. Blood, flesh, fire, water. Holy men and unholy consorts. She saw momentary depravities, and heard desperate, urgent whispers of dark truths and blasphemous lies. She felt the intensity of lust incarnate at her breast, a feeling so powerful that she gasped and dropped the card to the table. He released her wrist and the sensations ceased. He was watching her, and she saw cruelty in his amusement at her discomfort.

"Do tell," he said.

"I see lust," she replied, still breathless from the sensory torrent. "Pride, and—"

He raised a heavy eyebrow. "Go on."

"A fall into darkness." She felt her brow furrow. "I see ... Damnation."

He pursed his lips and stroked his substantial beard in contemplation of her summary. Mara noticed that his eyes had darkened, and with it his general demeanour.

"Have I offended you, sir?" she asked out of politeness, for in truth she did not care about his feelings either way.

"Not at all," he replied quietly, "I am honoured to have received your reading. As to its accuracy ... We shall have to wait and see what the fates decide, shall we not?"

"All things move toward their end," Mara replied.

He raised his glass to her sentiment and then drank it dry.

"You know, it is odd. I have refrained from drinking wine for some years," he said, regarding the empty glass, "until our meeting." Then he turned the glass over and placed it down upon its rim. It stained the white tablecloth with a red circle, which he studied thoughtfully as though it were some totem or emblem that only he could decipher. Mara waited. He emerged from his thoughts and stood up. He bowed his head to Mara in a gesture of flamboyant formality.

"I wish you a good appetite," he said, and then turned and stalked away.

Mara felt the air around her become clear of his intensity. Men such as he indulged their obsessions to the detriment of all around them. The waiter returned, bearing a dish of stale-looking pastries. She watched him make a fuss over pouring her tea. Even this manservant wanted her attention. Then the overbearing woman barked an order at him and he visibly flinched before administering to her demands.

Alone again at her table in the crowded car, Mara sighed, feeling lighter already. She ignored her breakfast and returned her attention to the tarot. No new diners were present and so she turned a final card for herself. *The Blasted Tower*. She knew it meant disaster, unrest, obstacles. The card's meanings were clear to her. Yet, she could not yet fathom why it had manifested itself upside-down. Inversion was such a difficult thread to unpick. The more you tugged at the implications, the more they became unravelled to the reader. Mara was contemplating such deeper meanings when the train lurched violently forward, and then back, slowing so suddenly that it flung the waiter against the aristocratic woman's table, spilling her tea. The aristocrat yelped in the manner of a startled animal and then struck the waiter with the flat of her hand.

Mara looked across at the window and noticed the Englishman mopping his brow. His face looked even paler than before, so much so that it appeared almost ghostlike. He glanced at her, then at the upturned wine glass on the table, before calling out to the waiter.

"I say. That fellow had wine! Why don't I have any bally wine?"

The train lurched again and the waiter moved away to look out of the window.

"I say! What's amiss?"

The Englishman rose, then swayed a little as he joined the waiter at the window.

From her table, Mara could see the gunmetal grey smear of the rock face giving way to the verdant green of massive fir trees, their branches heavy with snow and ice. At the head of the locomotive, the whistle blared.

Mara saw the hulking giant had remained seated at his table. He reached into his pocket and pulled out a fob watch. He studied it for a few moments and then snapped it shut. The click of the casing coincided with the noisy arrival of the train's conductor, his face red and slick with sweat beneath his cap. The conductor spoke animatedly with the maître d', whose eyebrows raised, registering surprise. The conductor finished speaking, breathless, and the maître d' nodded sagely before clearing his throat and then striding to the centre of the dining car.

"Distinguished guests," he intoned, in a thick Romanian accent, "due to signal, we make unscheduled stop at Bistritz."

"For how long?" The voice of the stranger from behind the shadow of his high collar was surprisingly melodic.

"I am afraid we do not know this, until our driver has spoken with the stationmaster," the maître d' said officiously.

"Oh bother," the Englishman said. "I have a connection to make at the Port of Constanta. At this rate I'll bally well miss it. Daresay we all will." He looked to his fellow travellers for a response. Receiving none, he exclaimed, "Only one thing for it then. Brandy!" He waved at the waiter.

"Perhaps there will be something that is actually edible at the station," the obnoxious aristocrat retorted from her table, which lay cluttered with rejected dishes. "Clear this mess away!"

Mara watched the waiting staff hurry to the woman's table, piling up dishes and cutlery. She scooped her tarot cards back into their silk scarf wrapper and tied it securely. All the while she noticed that the huge American remained quiet, those bright eyes of his twinkling, taking in the landscape through the window beside him. He looked completely unfazed by the delay, unlike the top-hatted stranger who had retreated so far into the shadows.

Mara winced at the deafening squeal of the train's great wheels as they slowed into Bistritz station. She watched engine smoke drift like an ominous fog over the slatted wooden timbers of station sheds – the first buildings she had seen in what felt like an age. The snowy treeline receded, and the locomotive crawled to a halt beside the platform. Gusts of wind cleared the smoke away, revealing the peeling paint of a sign:

"BISTRITZ"

Quiet fell over the car as the train staff busied themselves removing the dining things. Mara saw the conductor sweating and puffing his way past the window, clutching onto his hat in the rising wind. Another man emerged from a doorway set back from the platform edge. He looked like he had been sleeping in his uniform, was straightening it as he approached the conductor. The two spoke at length, both glancing nervously toward the front of the train. They seemed to reach an agreement; the stationmaster headed off toward the engine, and the conductor returned to climb aboard the train.

"Ladies and gentlemens," he said, "a landslide comes onto track before Borgo Pass. Not safe for travel any further. You must please to disembark."

CHAPTER TWO

The waiting room was a little warmer than the platform, at least.

The stationmaster had set a fire for his unscheduled new arrivals, although its glow had yet to reach beyond the grate. Mara pulled her heavy shawl tighter around her arms to keep the draught from her back. Glancing around at her fellow passengers, it struck Mara that such a collection of individuals could only meet while travelling. And now that the landslide had interrupted their journey they were collectively without a purpose. Since disembarking from the train, her fellow travellers had fallen into a prolonged silence as though it were subject to an unspoken agreement between them.

The aristocratic woman had perched herself on the wooden bench nearest the fireplace, her entire being poised in disgust at her surroundings. Beside her, the Russian holy man sat with his hands resting on his knees, gazing into the fire.

Reflected orange light danced in the pupils of his eyes, and Mara was reminded of the wolves that used to come at night to the treeline bordering the village where she grew up.

The Englishman paced up and down, more dog than wolf, and almost collided with Mara at one point. He apologised for his imposition, his breath thick with the scent of alcohol, and then retreated to the bench furthest from the door. Mara saw him slide a silver hip flask from inside his coat, then twist open the cap before taking a few sips too many.

Behind the Englishman, the high-collared stranger kept characteristically to the shadows beside a wall-mounted railway map.

The enormous American stood monolithic beside the draughty door, seemingly impervious to the cold.

The stationmaster despatched a boy carrying a tray of mugs and a carafe of hot coffee. The aristocrat made a show of her refusal, but Mara accepted a mug and made a point of depositing a coin on the tray in the boy's favour. The boy nodded his head politely and then waited for Mara to drink before offering her a welcome refill. The coffee was bittersweet and roasting hot – perfect for keeping the chill at bay. She placed her empty vessel on the tray and then smiled, seeing the boy biting into the silver coin before he carried the tray around the room, offering drinks to the men. The Englishman drank some of his coffee before topping it up from his hip flask. The stranger waved the boy away, those sharp eyes following the lad as he walked over to his final customer. The American towered over the boy and his tray. Mara saw him stoop, then whisper something in the lad's ear, before taking Mara's silver coin from the tray and flipping it. He caught the coin on the sleeve of his greatcoat and placed his enormous hand over it. Stooping again, he lifted his hand to reveal the coin to the boy, who looked dismayed. Without even studying the coin, the American pocketed it then ruffled the hair of the boy as he sloped out of the waiting room. Mara bit her lip, which was still warm from the coffee. A well-dressed adult playing a game of chance with a child of such meagre means. When she glanced back at the giant, she saw he was grinning. Mara was just about to address the brute when the stationmaster entered amid an icy blast of wind.

"We have secured accommodations for you," he announced. "A carriage awaits you, and then, a hot meal."

The American stepped out of the waiting room and Mara saw him stroll along the platform, gripping his wide-brimmed hat against the wind all the while. Do all Americans walk so purposefully, she wondered, as though they own the land beneath each and every footfall?

"What about our connections?" The Englishman always seemed to speak in terms of his schedule.

"The landslide has made the track impassable. The storms that caused it have kept all ships anchored at Constanta. Rest assured, you shall be able to continue your onward journey when all is clear once more." The stationmaster peered over his spectacles at the Englishman, getting the measure of him before adding, "For now, you will be able to fortify yourselves in comfort."

The Englishman's ears indeed pricked up at this. "And where are these fortifications, dear fellow?" he asked.

"A castle in the mountains a few miles from here. You will be safe and comfortable away from the storm, there. The castle has stood indomitable against the elements for some centuries past, and shall no doubt remain for several more hence."

The haughty voice of the aristocrat piped up from the fireside. "And our luggage?"

"Shall travel with you. The porters are unloading it from the express as we speak."

Even the snobby woman seemed to find no fault in this. The Russian gallantly helped her to her feet and escorted her from the waiting room. Mara noted the care and attention he paid to the woman's every move. As her hand fell, no doubt aided by the weight of her ostentatious jewellery, onto the back of his hand Mara could almost feel the subtlety with which he guided the woman to the door, steering her like a domesticated animal yet giving her the impression that she was leading. He was evidently well versed in the art of gaining the trust of wealthy, elderly women.

"After you, madam." The Englishman's voice startled her from her observations. He beamed at Mara, his face rosy from drink, a flirtatious twinkle in his eye.

She fastened her woollens about her and made her way to the exit. Mara gasped as the black-clad stranger reached out and held the door open for her. She hadn't even noticed him move from the shadows. He was as quick and silent as a spider. She felt a shiver pass through her as she brushed past him and onto the windy platform. As she followed the other travellers along the platform she realised it was not the wind that had given her a chill, but rather the stranger's sharp eyes upon her.

The carriage waited, large, black, and ornate, beyond a weather-beaten fence at the side of a dirt track that was masquerading as a road. Atop the carriage Mara glimpsed the dark figure of a driver, clad in black robes and a thick fur hat that appeared to have been fashioned from bearskin. He held a whip aloft in one hand, while his other clutched the leather reins of four enormous jet-black horses. One of them snorted into the cold air, its breath becoming a plume of steam to rival even that produced by the engine of the train they had left behind at the platform. Two porters were busy heaving luggage over their shoulders and atop the carriage. As she approached, one of the porters put a bulky valise to one side and then assisted her onto the step leading inside the carriage.

The cabin felt claustrophobic, an effect accentuated by the American's girth. He was so vast that he took up nearly an entire seat within the carriage. Mara heard the aristocrat beside her tut loudly and then noticed that the American had not removed his hat. Nor did he look likely to. Mara thought of the boy and his coin again – her coin – and, seeing the thin smile on the American's face, she looked away.

The Englishman was last to enter the carriage and, ever effusive in his apologies, proceeded to jostle his way into the seat beside the hulking man. The American remained as still as a statue, giving his neighbour no quarter. The carriage rocked from side to side as railway porters finished lashing the travellers' luggage to its roof. When all was secure, Mara heard one of the men call out to the driver. There came the sharp report of a whip, and the carriage lurched forward into motion. Mara gripped the leather strap below the window beside her to steady herself. The terrain beneath the wheels of the carriage grew rougher as they drove on, causing the vehicle to buck as wildly as the horses that pulled it.

"Rupert Grayson," the Englishman announced, apropos of nothing. He held out his hand to the hulking American who regarded it in the manner of a cat studying its next meal, before enclosing it in his massive fist and then shaking it.

Grayson whimpered at the American's grip, and Mara heard the painful cracking of finger bones.

"Ernst Von Sammler," the American rumbled, before releasing Grayson's hand.

"American, what?" The Englishman's voice sounded strained. His face had turned white as a sheet. Wincing as he withdrew his hand, he then tucked it under his armpit.

Mara stifled a chuckle. The American's brute strength and German name were having quite the effect on the Brit.

"And with whom do I have the pleasure of travelling?" Grayson had directed his question at Mara, but the aristocratic woman answered first.

"Lady Sophia Waddesdon," she said.

To Mara, her name evoked both the mothball odour of old manor houses and the collective despair of put-upon waiting staff.

"Delighted," Grayson said and attempted to kiss Lady Sophia's hand. The coach lurched violently, and he nearly landed in a heap upon the venerable woman's lap. She slapped him away impatiently, tutting all the while as though at an unruly child.

Blushing, Grayson squeezed himself back in the seat beside the American. "I say. Rough terrain. Reminds me of my time in Afghanistan, only with fouler weather. Daresay you're used to it in the Wild West, eh, what? The terrain?"

The American neglected to answer, turning his sharp blue eyes to the window. Mara guessed that for him, the conversation was over.

"And you, fair lady? What is your moniker, if I may be so bold?"

"I am Mara," she said, and then, seeing that he was preparing to stand up for another attempt at a hand kiss, "Please, remain seated."

He blushed redder still and then attempted to make eye contact with the Russian.

"Grigori Yefimovich Rasputin." The bearded man said his name quickly, sounding eager for the chatter to be over. The Englishman swallowed and then fell silent. The holy man's demeanour was having the desired effect.

Grayson then glanced at the high-collared stranger. His eyes were closed beneath the rim of his hat, which he had not even removed for the journey. The Englishman whispered conspiratorially to his travelling companions, "Shan't bother asking him for his name. The bounder's asleep! How anyone could sleep on this rocking horse ride is beyond me—"

"I daresay more than a few things are," Lady Sophia spat.

Grayson chuckled awkwardly, and then fell mercifully silent once more.

Mara saw the top-hatted stranger's eyelids flicker. Perhaps he was in the throes of some dream. Or perhaps he had been listening to every word. The shadow of his face was inscrutable. Mara tore her gaze from its contained darkness.

Outside the window, the weather and the terrain became wilder still the farther they travelled. Mara felt the biting cold of the wind penetrating the shell of the carriage, despite the warmth of her fellow travellers' bodies around her. She could discern from the angle of the vehicle that they were travelling up a steep incline. Peering out of the window beside her, she immediately regretted her course of action upon seeing a vertiginous drop into deep, black nothingness. She heard the crack of the driver's whip once again and clenched her teeth as the carriage tipped alarmingly in the direction of the abyss. Tearing her eyes away from the window, she pushed her body back into the unyielding upholstery. Another crack of the whip and the carriage sped on, its velocity marked by the frenetic clatter of the horses' hooves on the rocky ledge along which they travelled.

After what felt like an age the land began to level out, and the coach with it, provoking Mara to risk another look out of the window. She saw that they had progressed away from the narrow mountain ledge and onto a dirt track. Shadows closed in around them, the carriage shrouded by dense forest either side. Wild creatures stirred at the clatter of the coach and the scent of the horses, and Mara saw yellow eyes glowering from the treeline. The low wail of wolves echoed across the treetops and Mara glanced at Rasputin, remembering how his eyes had reflected the fire in the station waiting room. This time, she found he had his eyes shut – in meditation, or sleep, she did not know.

"Hah! Hah!"

The driver urged his horses on, the whip cracking madly to make them gallop ever faster. Mara felt worry clutching at her breast. If the driver overran the horses they might become injured, or at least unable to maintain the pace for long. The idea of being stranded out there in the wilderness was almost more than she could bear. She could feel the tension from her travelling companions, too. An unspoken, almost primal silence had seized the interior of the carriage punctuated only by the noisy remonstrations of the driver as he punished the horses with whip crack after whip crack. Mara saw dark shapes outside, keeping pace alongside the carriage, and she realised the urgency in a heartbeat. A pack of wild wolves was chasing them down, their sleek bodies threatening in the half-light of the sun as it flickered behind storm clouds. Their yelps and cries hinted at the feral savagery that drove them on.

The horses thundered through the landscape, the carriage creaking and groaning like the timbers of some great sailing ship in a storm. The front wheel on Mara's side struck something hard – a rock perhaps – and she was nearly sent toppling to the floor as the carriage rocked with the impact. Gripping the window strap tight, she managed to stay in her seat. The Englishman began to make some glib comment about the quality of the roads in the Carpathians when he too seemed to notice the wolf pack pursuing them. That shut him up, and Mara felt grateful for that small mercy.

"On! Hah!" the driver shouted, the snap of his whip punctuating his cries.

Mara heard the snarls of the wolf pack and saw through the window that they were gaining. Impossible that they could run so fast. Their fangs flashed white and Mara felt sick to her stomach, imagining the gnawing hunger that must possess such beasts. *"We have safety in numbers child,"* her father used to say when she could not sleep for fear of the howls echoing around her childhood village. They numbered only six in the carriage, plus the driver, but he was vulnerable out in the open. If the wolves reached the horses—

A strange glow appeared up ahead. Mara squinted through the mud-flecked glass of the carriage window and saw a huge ring of what looked like blue flame, encircling the twisting dirt track as it emerged from the tree cover. The carriage thundered on, straight through this strange phenomenon, and Mara fancied that the carriage would catch alight from the weird flames. The opposite became fact, for no sooner had it passed through the strange blue barrier than the air inside the carriage seemed to cool discernibly. The effect was not dissimilar to that experienced when entering a cave on a hot summer's day. Mara leaned forward so that she might peer back at the flames and she saw the shapes of the wolves behind them. They had given up their pursuit of the carriage at last, perhaps spooked by the weird phosphorescence of those dancing flames.

"Did you see that?" she asked the Englishman, upon noticing that he too had been peering out of the window on his side.

"Marsh gas," he said. "Smell must have put their noses out of joint. Bally lucky for us, actually, with those damnable hounds scenting us."

Mara sighed, feeling relief seep into her bones.

Then she saw the castle.

High atop the rocks it loomed, indomitable, at the centre of the dark hoofprint of the Carpathian Mountains. A jagged row of treetops either side gave the impression of black teeth bared to the stormy sky. Feeling queasy at the height,

Mara lowered her gaze. Again, the track became vertiginous as the carriage traversed a narrow causeway that snaked on toward the castle. The sun, already dipping low over the mountains, broke the clouds and Mara saw its light reflected on the surface of a wide moat encircling the fortress. As the carriage drew nearer to the outer wall of the structure, she noticed that the wall itself was hewn from the very rock upon which the castle crouched, hunkered down like a vast, predatory animal. And now that preternatural creature of stone and mortar showed its jaws as, with the great clanking of unseen mechanisms, the enormous drawbridge began to descend over the moat.

The driver urged his horses on, not for one moment slowing the pace as they hurtled toward the descending drawbridge. Mara held her breath, frightened for a moment that they might actually plunge into the black, icy waters of the moat, but the drawbridge completed its descent with a mighty thud upon the ground. In a heartbeat the carriage was up and onto the heavy wooden bridge, the horses' hoof falls echoing off the sheer wall of the castle.

The carriage thundered into a stone courtyard which was flanked by high watchtowers, each bearing a single flaming torch. The flames danced in the wind, casting wild shadows across the entrance of the castle. The doors were enormous, studded by great bolts of iron and weathered by centuries of Carpathian storms. The driver reigned the horses in, hard, and they whinnied to a sharp stop. Mara held tight onto the leather window strap until she felt the carriage come to a standstill. Only then did she let out a long, controlled breath.

She glanced at the aristocratic woman who looked to be on the edge of her self-imposed decorum, dabbing at the perspiration on her brow with a lace handkerchief. The Englishman looked rather sweaty, too, and used his cravat to wipe his upper lip before rapping on the ceiling of the carriage and bellowing, "I say old chap, let us out, will you? There's a good fellow."

Awkward moments passed without any indication that the driver intended to hop down from his seat in order to open the door for his passengers, as would usually be the custom – anywhere but here.

"I formally retract my last statement," the Englishman blustered.

"Uncouth ruffian," the aristocrat muttered, each syllable dripping poison, and for a moment Mara could not tell if she was referring to the driver or the Englishman.

Rasputin slapped his hands down onto his robed knees and then stood up. He pulled at the window strap then reached out through the window and turned the door handle. When he opened it, cold mountain air rushed into the carriage, heavy with the scents of wet stone and evergreens.

To Mara, it smelled almost like home.

So why is it, she wondered, *that I feel so afraid here?*

CHAPTER THREE

Grayson lost his footing on the bottom step of the carriage.

He would have tumbled onto the flagstones below were it not for the burly attendants who caught him, mid-fall, and set him roughly down on dry land. They were brutes, these two, almost as impressive in stature as the American chap who had damn near broken his fingers with that handshake. He mumbled his thanks to the two men and then licked his dry lips. The rocking of the carriage had instilled a dizziness in him that he had not experienced since his last round of gin punch with his fellows at the bar of Lord Cardigan's clubhouse. What he wouldn't do for a glass or two now, what with the icy wind mounting a full-frontal assault upon his buttonholes.

Only then did he realise that the rough duo still had him in their clutches. Had they saved him from his fall, or had they been sent to restrain him? They did rather have the aspect of prison guards with their drab attire and pockmarked faces. Unpleasant memories of his time in the brig – well, times, to be exact – came back to him and he shivered at them as much as the cold.

"I say, you fellows, I'm quite all right now. No need to fuss. Put those load-bearing hands of yours to better use, eh, what?" He nodded meaningfully over to the luggage that was still strapped to the roof of the carriage.

They released their grip on his coat sleeves, and he breathed the free air again. The coach horses whinnied and snorted as the burly men approached the carriage, muttering in the local dialect in their low voices. Grayson's ample experience in the saddle told him the steeds were in dire need of a watering. He was about to have a word in the ear of the driver but one of the attendants blocked his way. Not wishing to get into a disagreement with the locals, he beat a dignified retreat to the stone steps that led up to the (altogether impressive, he had to admit) castle doors.

He made way for the Russian escorting Lady Sophia up the steps. Grayson didn't much care for the holy man. He had fine whiskers, undoubtedly, but his hair could do with a trim. And Grayson's many manoeuvres into foreign territories had taught him never to trust a chap wearing robes. Lady Sophia was another beast entirely, of course. Formidable woman, that one. Her demeanour told Grayson that she must have been something of a firebrand in her youth, and he regretted not meeting her at a social when she was younger. He would have been but a teenager back then, of course. But no matter – he had cut his adult teeth, so to speak, on fine fillies like her. A few choice lines of poetry on a moonlit walk (away from the prerequisite stuffy old husband) had always served him well.

He recalled the night of his seventeenth birthday when a certain landed baroness had seemed hell-bent on becoming lost in her own garden maze with him. He had certainly walked out of those hedgerow walls a different man. Feeling a rush of warmth from such nostalgia, Grayson's eyes wandered again and found the young fortune teller. He savoured her lithe form as she moved, catlike, up the steps after the lady and her escort. Sometimes, he mused, it really was worth getting the occasional scratch, even at the risk of a flea in one's ear. He would have to circle that particular prey carefully.

Then he remembered seeing her reading tarot cards for the holy man and began to wonder if they were in cahoots. Come to think of it, he had noticed something of a dark look pass between the pair of them in the carriage. He watched them now and began to chuckle inwardly as he realised the sly fellow's game. He was evidently using Lady Sophia to get closer to the young woman. They both seemed to be cut from the same dark cloth, so he was being extra careful to show decorum, and to demonstrate what a fine gentleman he was. No doubt he would widen his circle of gentlemanly influence as the evening wore on, and draw closer to the actual hand that he intended to kiss. Grayson had seen operations such as this in the field and, in matter of fact, he had orchestrated a fair few of them himself. He decided to remain on the outskirts of the battlefield for now, as was his preference anyway. If the dark fellow overstepped the mark, he would be waiting in the wings to step in – ever the gentleman, naturally – and "save the day". Then the fortune teller would be warm putty in his hands.

For now, Grayson had other desires to satiate. His sharp sense of smell had picked up a delicious olfactory trace of what could only be roast meat. The burly fellows opened the huge doors upon an enormous foyer, flanked by high stone stairwells and an arched ceiling so high it almost had a vanishing point. Grayson followed his nose, and his fellow travellers, inside. The attendants closed the doors against the elements behind them, and all was cool and quiet within that vast foyer.

"Follow," said one of the men in a low voice, and then led them through a passageway that ended in double doors. These, the attendants flung open with a flourish, revealing the source of the delectable smell of food. The silent group filed into a great hall, elegantly lit with candles in cast-iron candelabras. At its centre stood an enormous table laden with a feast so vast that its legs must surely be buckling beneath it. The spread was a veritable marvel, boasting cuisine from all across the British Empire and far beyond. Grayson's eyes began to bulge as they took it all in.

At the head of table sat a dark fellow in queer robes that looked more Far Eastern than Eastern European to Grayson's well-travelled eye. He sat stoic, as if entranced, which was more than understandable given the feast laid out before him.

"Chap has more willpower than I do," Grayson said to the others, as much to break the silence in the feasting hall than anything. "I would have tucked in by now."

In truth, a dog in season had more willpower than he could muster at this particular time.

"I say, is this seat taken?" Grayson chuckled, but the queer-looking fellow remained completely silent. "Bally rude of you, sir. There are ladies present!"

Perhaps their host was waiting for them to take their seats? An archaic dining custom in these parts, perhaps. Either that or the poor fellow was a deaf mute. Or had taken leave of his senses, which was what Grayson feared might happen to him if he didn't commence mastication immediately.

"I say, it's as though they bally well knew I was coming," he said, encircling the table to feast his eyes upon some exquisite looking crystal bowls of crème brûlée. "Not only do they have my favourite roast venison, but my absolute tip-top dessert of choice." He could not resist cracking a topping with his index finger, and tasting the sweetness from within. Extraordinary. "Bravo to the chef!" he exclaimed, his appetite well and truly whetted.

Salivating at the prospect of tucking into the succulent roast venison, Grayson licked his lips and then sat down, keeping an empty seat between himself and the rude fellow in the robes. It had not passed Grayson's notice that there were just enough seats for him and his fellow travellers, plus one, which remained empty.

"So strange. They have a goulash here that I have never seen outside of my village," Mara murmured, seemingly as intoxicated by the scent rising from the bowl as Grayson was by that of the roast. "It smells exactly how I remember it, wild woodland herbs and all."

Grayson watched as she sat down and dipped a silver spoon into the bowl before taking a taste. A shiver of pleasure seemed to pass through her body; *what a minx*, he thought. She sighed heavily and then muttered in a dialect he could not quite place. He saw that she had tears glistening in the corners of her eyes and recalled feeling precisely the same way about his first Yorkshire pudding after a lengthy spell in the Crimea.

"You may keep to your peasant food, young lady," Lady Sophia deadpanned. "I shall avail myself of this delicious roast pheasant."

Rasputin assisted her with her chair – the sly dog – and then she looked around as if awaiting the arrival of some personal butler to carve the bird for her. But the burly men had retreated to the shadows encircling the table.

"How strange that you manage to maintain such a wealth of ingredients and culinary expertise so high up in the mountains. Allow me to compliment your kitchen staff on a most exquisite luncheon," Lady Sophia proclaimed.

Still, the queer fellow in the robes remained oblivious to their presence. Grayson spied the odd man's lips moving, ever so slightly. It was as though he were whispering words that only he could hear.

Lady Sophia harrumphed in disgust at the man's ignorance. "I daresay your kitchen staff have better manners, sir!"

The American giant sat opposite Grayson and plucked a dish of refried beans from the centre of the table. He lifted the dish to his chest and began to fork the food into his mouth mechanically. He would have looked equally at home dining beside a campfire, such was the sorry state of his table manners.

Hovering beside the table like the shadow cast from one of the candelabras, the high-collared stranger reached out and took a silver knife from an empty place setting. He used it to spear a slice of beef, which he ate from the tip of the knife, like a dog, before retreating to the recess of an arched window, away from his fellow diners.

Rasputin sat down at the head of the table opposite their silent host and poured a large flagon of wine. He took a sip and then Grayson saw him carefully studying the goblet, which was exquisitely cast in the shape of a dragon, its stem the coiled tail of the beast.

Presently, Grayson heard shuffling footsteps over the sound of his laboured chewing. His cummerbund was already straining from the amount of tucker he had forced down into his belly, and he attempted to loosen it for fear he might belch at any moment. *And what would Lady Sophia have to say about that? It doesn't bear thinking about, the old battle-axe.* The footsteps grew nearer and a man entered the great hall. He walked with a stoop and his breathing laboured with each step as though he were carrying some significant yet invisible weight upon his rounded shoulders. His face was pallid, his eye sockets so deep and shadowed that he could perhaps be four score years old, yet his shock of jet-black hair suggested otherwise.

"My master bids you welcome," he said in a thin voice, which was really no more than a whisper. Each laboured vowel sound marked him as native to this mountainous region. "I am Klove, and I am at your service."

Despite this admission of his servant status, the strange fellow sat down at the table in the empty chair. Perhaps another queer custom of this region, yet Grayson thought it most unlikely.

"I trust you have enjoyed your luncheon?" Klove rasped.

Grayson heard a choke of outrage emanating from Lady Sophia's throat.

"The quality of the food, I admit, is exquisite," she said, her voice as clipped as a topiary sculpture. "The conversation offered by our host, however, leaves much to be desired."

The butler's eyes followed Lady Sophia's glare to the silent, robed figure seated at the head of the table.

"Host?" he asked, then let out a wheezing chuckle from somewhere deep within his cadaverous frame. "Host! Oh no, my dear lady, this gentleman is another of our esteemed guests. He arrived … shortly before you did."

The robed figure remained silent, staring at some imperceptible detail upon the dining table. He had the air of a wanderer about him and it was as though those shadow-rimmed, staring eyes of his had seen far too much on his travels.

Grayson noticed Lady Sophia's glare sharpen to a near murderous point, and how tightly she gripped her fork in one liver-spotted fist! He would have to get to know her with expediency. She was mere blood vessels away from leaving some lucky fellow her estate.

"Now that you have dined, some entertainment," Klove announced.

Perhaps he was imagining things, but Grayson thought he saw the butler glance darkly at the burly henchmen, as though giving them the silent nod.

"We shall play a parlour game. Each of you will now be shown to your room. You will find instructions about our amusing little game there. If you each play along satisfactorily, you will be free to go in the morning."

"Sounds bally mysterious to me," Grayson said, hoping that his quarters were within seducing distance of the fortune teller's so that he might suggest pooling their efforts.

"I do not play along with such childish games," Rasputin remarked.

Klove levelled his gaze at the Russian and, for a moment, the eyes beneath the mop of black hair took on a more sophisticated aspect. He licked his thin lips.

"Oh, but you shall. And one more thing. Only one of you may leave."

"I say, steady on old chap," Grayson said.

"What is the meaning of this?" Lady Sophia countered. Her voice seemed to have lost some of its resolve. A frisson of fear passed around the dining table making the guests shiver as though from a cold draught.

"Only one of us? Sir, kindly explain yourself." Mara's voice, too, was strained, but she held firm with a dignity beyond her years.

Fine young filly, that one, thought Grayson.

Klove simply smiled, those thin lips holding onto their secrets.

"You jest," Rasputin protested.

"I assure you, dear sir, this is no jest. You will now be taken to your quarters."

"I refuse to bow to the will of any other. No man may command me, least of all some Romanian lackey!" Rasputin bellowed. And, pushing his chair back so violently as he stood up it nearly toppled over, he added, "Out of my way!"

As the holy man strode toward the door Klove nodded to the attendants, who snapped into position, blocking his exit from the room. Rasputin appeared to measure them up and then turned on his heel, protesting, as he strode instead to the largest of the arched windows on the other side of the hall.

"I will swim across the moat to freedom if I have to!" he roared.

"Please, be our guest," Klove said, before nodding to his men again, quite openly this time.

They closed in around Rasputin, seizing him in their strong arms. The outraged Russian lashed out at them, his long hair flapping like a war banner on a battlefield, but they were too many – and too strong for him. Grayson and the women alike gasped at what they saw next. One of the attendants reached out and unfastened the huge leaded window, flinging it open wide. Shock then registered on Rasputin's face as the men lifted him from his feet. Without any word of warning, they hurled him out of the window, backwards.

Mara rushed over to the window, careless of the threat of the brutes who stood there admiring their grim handiwork as the holy man plummeted to earth. An almighty splash erupted far below as Rasputin hit the water. Grayson finished his glass of port to steady his nerves then ambled over to the window, cautious of the attendants who still stood there, panting from their murderous exertions.

He looked down and realised just how far the Russian had fallen. Ripples on the moat's dark surface marked the spot where he had entered the cold murk.

"Help him! Help him, you monsters! He will drown!" Mara's cry was one of complete empathy for the fallen holy man.

It seems the old fellow certainly endeared himself to her during their card game aboard the train, Grayson thought. He looked to Rasputin's other dalliance, and found Lady Sophia's countenance to be quite pale. He sidled closer to her so that he might be the one to catch her if she should faint. Then Mara screamed, and Grayson looked down from the window again to see Rasputin reappear. His anguished face broke the surface of the moat, his skin plastered with fronds of black hair like waterweeds.

"By gad!" Grayson exclaimed. "Chap's survived!"

He watched as the poor fellow opened his mouth wide, taking air into his shocked lungs while moving his arms in circles to keep himself afloat. He appeared injured and in some considerable distress. His right arm, Grayson noted, was moving less than the left, the Russian's drenched garment torn all about it. Those dark eyes looked up at the window pointedly, as though conveying silent curses to the watchers above. Then, he wheeled around in the drink and began swimming – awkwardly due to his injured arm – toward the water's edge. Grayson saw the bankside of the moat was sheer, and looked damnably slippery to boot. *A fellow would have to be Spring-Heeled Jack to scale it, if it could be done at all*, he thought.

Then, Grayson realised the extent of Rasputin's plan. He was swimming diagonally across the dark channel of the moat toward the mechanism of the drawbridge. Even though the bridge was shut, the huge chains that powered it hung tantalisingly above the surface of the water. The fellow was made of stern stuff, that much was certain, but the distance from water to chain looked considerable. And then there was the not insignificant matter of the man's injured arm to take into consideration. It was a rum business, survival against those odds. *All things considered, and with no offence implied,* Grayson thought, *I might not be betting in this chap's favour.*

Grayson heard a thin, mocking cackle, which roused him from his thoughts. He saw quiet delight on Klove's face as he watched Rasputin's efforts. That quick tongue licked at those thin lips once more and Grayson detected an unsavoury hunger within the gesture.

I say, something else is wrong here, he thought. *By the pricking of my thumbs, very wrong indeed.*

No sooner had he thought it than Grayson saw the surface of the water shift darkly, mere feet away from Rasputin's legs. Seemingly oblivious to this threat the Russian was paddling bravely on, toward the nearest hanging chain. The water had to be freezing, and for that alone Grayson admired the fellow's resolve. But that disturbance in the water was moving toward Rasputin, and picking up speed.

Mara gasped, another scream dying in her throat. Lady Sophia's eyes widened, bulging in denial at nature's transgression playing out before her in the moat below. The water swelled beneath Rasputin, rising wavelike. And the holy man rose too, his body lifted slightly by the swell – and perversely, closer to the drawbridge – before it enveloped him utterly in its unfathomable, wet blackness.

Grayson caught one last glimpse of Rasputin's pained visage, the profile of a drowning man, before it was dragged under by some unseen force. All but one hand disappeared beneath the water. Rasputin's hand clawed at the unforgiving surface, a devastatingly futile gesture against the inevitable. And then the hand too was gone, lost beneath the fatal wave, which rolled back, erasing all trace that there had been a human being there just moments ago.

Klove snapped his fingers and his henchmen closed and latched the window, sealing them all to their fate.

Rasputin's murderers turned to face their shocked guests, their emotionless eyes seeking out any further rebellion. Grayson looked to the American, expecting him to retaliate, but the huge man stood down, a sheep in wolf's clothing.

Grayson knew when to bow out gracefully, and did so now under the pretence of helping Lady Sophia back to her seat. Mara appeared to cling to a moment's defiance before she too retreated from the threatening men and their dark smiles.

"Now. We will show you to your rooms," Klove said, as casually as someone who had just served the after-dinner liqueur. "Please do remember that the castle is old, and its stonework uneven. Accidents can happen if you are not careful. Attend your escorts closely, and tread with care so that no harm may befall you. When you are in your rooms, you will find further instructions for the evening's entertainment."

Klove insinuated his unpleasant presence beside Lady Sophia, who was in something of a swoon. He put himself directly in between her and Grayson, then took her hand.

The absolute bounder, thought Grayson, *he's acting as though he were a suitor-in-waiting, not some peasant butler!*

"Come, dear lady, I will assist you to your room," he wheezed in that peculiar, high-pitched voice of his.

Well, the old girl must have been in shock, because she complied without as much as a murmur of protest or insult. In more civilised climes, Grayson would be summoning despatches. As it was, he kept mum, especially as one of the henchmen had appeared at his side – a dark cloud obscuring an already forgotten sun.

Grayson watched, tense, as Klove led Lady Sophia away to a recessed doorway flanked by enormous tapestries. The butler glanced over his shoulder and said, "Heed my words. You must follow the rules of the game to the letter. Until morning, I bid you all farewell," before leaving shock and confusion in his wake.

The sight of the holy man's hand slipping beneath the moat's black waters haunted Grayson. He dared not put a foot wrong in this accursed castle. Whatever dark game was afoot here, Grayson needed to keep his wits about him. Only one thing for it.

"One moment old boy," Grayson said, attempting to disguise the tremor in his voice.

He refilled his goblet to the brim with port wine and began quaffing it, even as the burly man led him out of the hall. As he stepped out into the clammy chill of the corridor, Grayson felt the old tremor in his drinking hand and wished he had brought the whole damned bottle along with him.

CHAPTER FOUR

He followed the henchman along the gloomy passageway, and wondered if this was Hell.

The nameless wanderer's mind was a blank, a fathomless void that echoed his complete lack of memory about this place. He had no recollection of how he had even come to be at this dreary castle. The others who had arrived after him had offered no clues, their language indecipherable and their mannerisms utterly alien to him. He knew that his darker skin and silent demeanour had cast him as an outsider in their eyes. And, as he had absolutely no idea from whence he had originated, an outsider he would remain. He attempted to process all that he had witnessed thus far. The unappetising meal, the unwelcome company, and the cold, casual murder of one of their number.

Each passageway, each stairwell and corridor, looked the same to him. He had no recollection of coming to this place. He knew not what this place was to him. The people he had met in the great hall had seemed to him mere phantoms, faceless players in some convoluted theatre of his fractured mind.

He drew his robes tighter around his body against the cold and tried to take solace in the fact that the chill in his bones felt real. If this was Hell, he surmised, then Hell must be a terribly cold place after all. The henchman led him round a corner and up to a heavy wooden door, which he opened with an unceremonious grunt, before showing him inside a room.

He entered and glanced around at the sparse furnishings – a single bed against one wall, a small chest and a chair near a narrow, leaded window. Hearing the door shut behind him he glanced back and heard a key turn in the lock. He was locked in, alone, and how he felt about that he did not know.

Crossing to the window, he peered through the dirty glass to see the sharp drop of a mountainside below. Had there been mountains where he had come from? He searched his heart for any recognition, but found nothing, only a hollow sense of never having really lived at all until he had come here. His eyes followed a dark line that curved through the trees and described the progress of a road leading up to the castle. Had he wandered here on foot? He looked down at his grubby, sandaled feet. Perhaps. Was that all he was, a nameless, stateless wanderer, doomed forever to walk in an alien and hostile place without an inkling as to how he had arrived? His head was a boiling cauldron of fear, of anger, and confusion. How could he not know anything about himself or his surroundings? How could he not remember!?

The wanderer leaned his forehead against the glass. It too was cold to the touch and he tried to focus on its reality, to place himself within some context of this castle. Yet try as he might to remember something – anything – all he felt was an overwhelming and sudden fatigue, sapping what little strength remained in his bones.

He retreated to the bed and found a scroll of paper atop the pillow. It was sealed, with some winged creature he did not recognise embossed within the red wax. Breaking the seal, he unfurled the paper and studied it. The text was foreign to him, its meaning utterly imperceptible. Why could he not understand!? He balled the paper in his frustrated fist and let it drop to the floor beside the bed. Curling into a foetal position on his side with his back to the locked door he felt something approaching relief as sleep took him down into its velvety depths.

***

A sharp click awoke him, and he rubbed sleep from his eyes. He knew not how long he had slumbered, but saw that the grey skies outside the narrow window had turned black from night's kiss. Hearing a creak from behind him, he rolled over and saw that the door was now open. He got up from the bed and stretched his cold, aching limbs. Then, the cryptic note at his feet already forgotten, he straightened his robes and stole out into the passageway.

In search of answers.

CHAPTER FIVE

Cold tears of fear stung Lady Sophia's eyes as she followed Klove, reluctantly, along the corridor.

She kept replaying the cruel murder of Rasputin at the hands of the man who now guided her to whatever fate she dared not imagine. Moments before she had swooned, she had heard Rasputin's hoarse cry from the moat as his head had broken the surface of the water. That cry seemed to echo on even now, freezing her bones with dread as though it were she who had plunged to her death in the cold, uncaring waters. The tears at the corners of her eyes were akin to a veil of ice that clouded her view. As Klove led her round a sharp bend in the corridor, she stumbled, and had to catch her fall against the stone wall, itself so cold and slimy to the touch.

"Mind your step, dear lady," Klove said in that sinuous whisper of his.

Lady Sophia recoiled as he reached for her arm, his grip around her wrist as absolute as a spider's around its prey.

"Come," he whispered, "your room is not far from here."

Lady Sophia would usually put a fellow like this in his place, yet she felt so very afraid of this man. Twice thus far she had almost lost her footing on the damnably uneven stone flags that passed for flooring in this accursed backwater castle, and twice her chaperone had failed to prevent her fall until the very last moment. It was entirely as though this monster meant for her to meet her maker, face down in some gloomy corridor at the back-end of beyond. And yet, his touch was abhorrent to her. With his strange stoop and peculiar voice, he had the aspect of a clerical worker, or lowly butler, about him. Not simply the dubious kind, who would serve you reheated leftovers and do it with a smile, but one with murderous intentions. She had met scores of parasites such as Klove in her time on this unforgiving earth, but none that possessed this fellow's brazen wickedness. She shuddered again at the memory, still starkly real in her mind's eye, of Rasputin's murder. The stooped man beside her was a cold-blooded killer, this much was certain. He had proven himself capable of being party to fell deeds. Even without his heavy-handed henchmen, his very presence was threatening.

Lady Sophia felt her chest tighten and her breath quicken as they rounded yet another corner that led into yet another dank corridor. She felt a damp chill prickling the skin where her neck met her collar. The draught emanated, she noted with dismay, from a cracked windowpane. Granted, the castle must have several windows, but the poor quality of upkeep was really quite unacceptable. To what manner of place had she been delivered!? Her sharp eyes began to notice every chipped flagstone, every leak in the ceiling – each and every fault in this godforsaken, joyless place. As she had often been at great pains to explain to her own lackadaisical estate staff, wealth was nothing without the correct cultural artefacts to demonstrate one's nobility.

Lady Sophia began to wonder what even passed as "nobility" in these wild, anarchic lands. She peered at Klove's tatty butler's uniform and noted with additional dismay that it was wearing thin at the elbows. Doubtful that his employer even knew the importance of such things. Warlords and robber barons, she suspected, the lot of them, their only claim to a title the result of some brutal act of aggression or another. Not like her proud bloodline with its estate becoming a duty of care for each successive generation. Unlike the barbarians in these inhospitable parts, at least her beloved British Empire had the decency to display its spoils in museums for the education and enjoyment of all. After liberating them from savages like this brigand, of course. These bare walls and chilly corridors spoke only of a last, and rather dismal, line of defence. Who would live in such a ghastly place?

Her heart was in her mouth with trepidation at being led deeper into this castle, and further into its darkness. Her hand moved to her throat and she absentmindedly clutched at the silver locket that hung there above her heart. How she wished her husband could be here to protect her. How she wished that things could have worked out differently. She realised with a jolt that she had not given Archibald a single thought since that morning. She opened her locket and looked at the face of the man to whom she owed so much. Archibald had been her sixth husband and by far her favourite, God rest his soul. She closed the locket and then tucked it back into her clothing. It felt cold as the grave against her skin after being exposed to the castle's dank atmosphere.

"Your room," Klove announced, before standing still next to a rather unimpressive looking door. He stood back to allow Lady Sophia to approach, but she remained rooted to the spot in terror, afraid of taking another step closer to Rasputin's killer.

"Ah," he said, before lurching forward and opening the door for her.

The musty odour that greeted her nostrils told her that the room had not been properly aired for quite some time. It was dark inside, terrifyingly so, and she had to clear her throat twice – and loudly – before Klove carried his lantern into the room. He opened the little glass door of the lantern and then used a taper to light a single meagre candle that stood on a dresser opposite the bed. The flickering candlelight revealed that it was no four-poster. In fact, it did not look like an acceptable bed at all, but rather somewhere that an animal might sleep.

"Please do come in," Klove whispered.

Lady Sophia trembled in her fear, and stayed in the corridor beyond the doorway. Klove fixed her with an emotionless gaze and she felt another cold tear of terror betray her as it trickled down her cheek. Then, his face rearranged itself into the approximation of a smile, like the one he had worn at luncheon, before he stepped out of the room and then aside to allow her entry.

"I trust you will be comfortable, dear lady," Klove said.

Avoiding his eyes, Lady Sophia rushed past him and into the room, slamming the door shut behind her. Her trembling fingers found the key and turned it in the lock with such force it felt as though it might snap off in her hand. She waited, breath caught in her throat, until she heard Klove's footsteps, along with his low chuckle, fading away to silence.

She was alone.

Turning her attention to the room she found it to be her worst nightmare made real. First and foremost was the odour, stronger now she was shut inside, and safe, she hoped. A dank smell permeated every inch of the room, the taint of mould on the fabrics and the grime of decades coating every surface. The candle, a peasant's tallow stump, sputtered in a cracked washbowl atop a decrepit table, adding the stench of animal fat to the room's already foul and noxious air.

As her eyes adjusted to the dim candlelight, she felt bile rise to her throat upon seeing clumps of straw poking out from beneath the threadbare blanket that lay atop the single bed.

Curiously, a scroll of paper lay upon the pillow, sealed with red wax. Such perversity, to leave any such welcome for a guest in these hellish quarters! Lady Sophia crossed to the bed and winced as she heard a dead bug crunch beneath her heel. Recoiling in horror from the stomach-churning squishing sound, she lost her balance on the uneven flagstones and toppled over. The straw mattress broke her fall and she clung to it for dear life, panting in anxious relief that she had not struck her head upon the flagstones of this locked room.

She attempted to calm her breathing and to regain her composure. Her gaze fell once more upon the scroll of paper that lay upon the pillow. Its wax seal, the only opulence to speak of in this dismal place, bore the emblem of a dragon in flight. Intrigued, she picked up the scroll and then shrieked as a monstrous spider scurried out of it. She shook the scroll and the spider landed on the bed before scuttling away on its black, hairy legs. Moving away from the bed, and closer to the candlelight, she snapped the wax seal and unrolled the paper. The hand that had inscribed it had been elegant indeed, the ink a ruby colour so dark that it was almost black in hue.

"You ..." it read, *"I know what you have done. Tonight, a reckoning is at hand. Know that only one shall leave this place. For the others, damnation awaits. Should you slay a fellow guest, bring proof to my tower and you shall be rewarded. If you choose a coward's path then pray to whatever gods you worship, but know they will not save you. For I hold dominion in this cursed place and your fate is all but sealed.*

Your friend, D."

Lady Sophia trembled, and bit her lip against frightful tears that were once more forming in the corners of her eyes. Her fate seemed to be sealed, just as the note said. But who was "D"? And what madness would give cause to set honoured guests one against the other? If any among their number was frail and vulnerable, it was she. Her advancing years were altogether a disadvantage, and her only potential ally and protector had been murdered in cold blood. Dash it all! She sat down upon the corner of the makeshift bed and allowed the tears to come. Fate had dealt her a bad hand indeed. How long would she wait, all alone in this filthy room, before someone came to "slay" her? She stared at the locked door in bitter dread, imagining that it might be broken down at any moment.

An eternity of such dread seemed to pass before she realised that she had crushed the scroll in her hand. She looked at the crumpled paper and its broken wax seal. Her fingers were white where she had clenched them so tight. And around the ring finger of her left hand, her wedding band gleamed, a white-gold beacon of hope that reminded her of her husband, of the stately home he had left to her in his last will and testament, and of her station in life. Despite her advancing years, and any such outward frailty, she still possessed the inner strength to persevere, to live! She conjured the faces of her fellow travellers in her mind's eye. Not one of them was fit to open a door for her. She was their superior, not only in breeding but also in intellect.

Remember who you are, she told herself.

Lady Sophia stood up, and wiped the tears from her eyes on the lace cuffs of her dress. She must remain true to her surname, to the proud bloodline of her beloved. Her family crest was prouder and more indomitable than any foreign nobleman's wax seal. All that she had endured and the sometimes difficult decisions that she had never hesitated to make were testament to her persistence. She was, and ever had been, a survivor and so she knew she must now establish a plan for her survival.

Remember ...

She thought of the place she felt safest, visualised it as though she were standing in it, there and then. She closed her eyes and remembered the sweet smell of lavender from the herb gardens, drifting in through the open window. Birdsong from the orchard lifted her heart as it had done on many a summer's morning. Her bedroom, at her manor. That was where she wished to be, above all else.

Opening her eyes, she grimaced at the disgusting servant's room and its filthy bed, the stark opposite to her beautiful boudoir in England. She knew now what she must do in order to survive. It was, after all, what she had done for most of her life; retreat to a place of comfort, of opulence, and safety, and wait it out in luxury while the underclasses fought among themselves.

Now that she had found her resolve, she would seek lodgings in this castle befitting her status, then barricade herself in with a four-poster bed and a decanter of fine wine.

Lady Sophia took the candle and walked to the door, careless now of any bugs that she might crush underfoot.

CHAPTER SIX

*H*e thinks he has the measure of me, this brute.

The way he saunters and swaggers, his shoulders so broad they almost scrape the sides of the narrow corridor as he leads me a merry dance, deeper into it. But I know dark places. I have mapped their interior until they have become as familiar to me as the back of my black-gloved hand. The dimly gas-lit streets of Whitechapel are not such a far cry from the narrow passages of this castle. Torchlight flickers and I notice the sweat pooling under my guide's stained short collar. I hear the laboured, heavy breath borne of a diet of cheap cuts and too many potatoes. As we descend some steps he puffs and pants like the fat old landlord from The Ten Bells back home. He even has to steady himself by placing one of his massive hands against the wall as he reaches the bottom step. And as he does so, I see it glint at his belt. The tip of the blade looks invitingly sharp, the silver of it brighter than a full moon over the Thames. It's an assassin's blade, designed for quick despatch into the hereafter. I have wielded many like it in my time, and shall again. The fingers of my knife hand twitch uncontrollably in the direction of the blade's hilt—

Not yet.

I must find my moment. He's overweight, yes, and out of shape. But he looks strong, too, let's not underestimate that. Strong enough to hurl that Russian into the moat. One down, four to go, until I'm the last man standing. And with that thought firmly front and centre in my mind, I keep the dazzling assassin's blade in the periphery of my vision, and begin assessing the pressure points beneath the fatty folds of the goliath's lumbering body.

He leads me on, into the very bowels of the castle, and I begin to wonder if he intends to lay me low in some dead end. Let him try. I stuck a deckhand once at Saint Katharine's Dock, and he was a similar size. Had the misfortune to cross me when my blood was up and went straight back to sea via the river, face down and eyes wide open, when I was done with him. This one in front of me now won't float. I'd probably do my back a mischief dragging him to a window so I could put him in the moat, like he did that poor Russian. He leads me round another corner and my mind wanders to the oily voice of the butler, Klove. All that Billy Bollocks about further instructions, and some kind of reward? It's meaningless to me. See, I've been biding my time all the while on the train, but now this – this is an opportunity to further my important work before I continue my journey.

They always say to love thy vocation. Roll your sleeves up and take pride in your toil, they say – and – life's too short, you never know how long you've got! When I roll my sleeves up, my cuffs get bloody all the same. I love my work, and take the utmost pride in it. It's my calling. No one knows I whistle while I work. In my head, at least. When I stick them, hard and fast, it's like nothing else. It's an act of mercy for the wretches.

The filth.

As I carve them, slow and steady with a surgeon's hand, I know I'm doing God's work!

They lie down dirty.

I raise them up clean.

When I grasp their inner secrets with my bare hands, it is an offering to a higher power. The lights go out in their grubby eyes and, yes, it's job satisfaction guaranteed. But it is over all too soon, and so I begin planning my next one before the blood has even dried on me.

My knife hand is twitching again in anticipation of the blade. It has been far too long since I experienced these sensations. Even the letters to plod had to stop for a while. But I know I'll find my inspiration again when I take another. Open her up. Reveal her dirty secrets. Make her clean again. Bodies are like envelopes. Only when I tear into them can I unpack their true meaning. That's the only reward I'm after.

"Here. Your room."

He's panting so hard he can barely get the words out. The sweat's fair pouring off him now, the poor sap! A door at the end of a narrow passage is lit by a single flaming torch that drips burning fat onto the stone floor. I savour the smell and lick my lips, remembering old tastes. Not long now. Moments, really. I watch him unlock the door, affecting disinterest. He gestures for me to step inside and I know that the time is now.

Now!

The knife is in my hand before he can even react and its blade is inside his belly a fraction of a second after that. His eyes widen, bulging like a constipated baby's. He begins to raise one massive fist in retaliation against my surprise assault. I push the blade further in, testing its sharpness, sampling its strength, and I don't stop until I feel its tip scrape against backbone. The fist drops, useless, to his side and he moans. His stomach is glove-warm around my hand. I can feel his weight bearing down on my hand as his knees buckle. His moan becomes a wet utterance of defeat. I give pause for a moment before the welcome sensation of release as I wrench the sharp sting of the blade out of his belly. His flesh undulates as his severed nerve endings try – and fail – to find connection within the rest of his organism. He stumbles backwards, a clumsy child, and slams into the wall. He slides to the floor, his massive body folding in upon itself. I watch red velvet lines form around the exit wound in his fat, yellow belly. He gurgles like a newborn, blood bubbling in his nostrils. I wonder how sharp the blade was that his midwife used to cut his umbilical when he was brought screaming into this world. Was it anywhere near as sharp as the one I have used to slice him a new one as he gurgles his way out of it?

Doubtful.

The craftsman who fashioned this particular weapon was skilled indeed.

I open my fist and weight the dagger in my hand. It is perfect balanced. I thrust it out into the wide-open possibility of the doorway in front of me. It is a perfect extension of my hand. Part of my being. I describe a circle with the silver tip and then hold the blade aloft in quiet salutation.

I feel whole again.

I am one with the blade.

I give it purpose. And the blade gives me meaning. We shall eviscerate our dark workings together this night, stalk the corridors of the castle until they are awash with the salt sweet scent of purpose and of meaning.

I am contemplating my first step into new discoveries when I make an unexpected one in an instant. Inside the room, upon the nightstand beside the bed, I spy a scroll of paper. It is as though the castle has been listening to my innermost thoughts. Perhaps it has. Oh, but I do feel at home in its dark embrace! Drawing the cloak of solitude around me, I tear into the seal just as I tore into my former guide. I read the contents, register their import, then screw them up and stuff them into the slathering mouth of the dead goliath.

Let them be his last words.

An epitaph.

I wipe his blood from the knife using first his greasy hair, and then the collar of his shirt. I hold it up to the torchlight once more. It gleams with the forensic simplicity of death over life.

Functional.

Beautiful.

So, it's to be a battle to the death, is it? We have work to do, this blade and I. And so, I set about it.

I retrace my steps so confidently that I might be taking a stroll through Limehouse itself. I am about to emerge into a wider corridor when I hear a sharp, female voice. Ducking back into the shadows, I listen as the voice draws near. It is unmistakably Lady Sophia's. I chance a look round the corner, confident that the cover afforded by the wall, along with that of my hat and greatcoat, will conceal me from view. Yes, there she is, with that slippery customer Klove beside her. I feast upon the fearful look in her eyes and feel my blood come up in an instant as I imagine the old sow's, decorating the dull stonework. I recall the contents of the note from the envelope. One thing truly does lead to another. Fate has placed into my path the first throat that I shall cut with this exquisite assassin's blade. First blood, Klove's henchman, was all too easy. Lady Sophia's noble blood will mark the evolution of an idea set into motion by my arrival in this place. Unseen in the shadows, I watch Klove guiding her on along the corridor.

As they proceed round another corner I insinuate myself into the night. And begin the hunt.

CHAPTER SEVEN

M ara kept as much distance between herself and the burly attendant as was possible in the confines of the corridor.

She felt the tight grip of anxiety about her person as he led her on. She knew that its source was the horrific sight of the poor Russian holy man, hurled from the window to his demise in the moat. Seeing him dragged like that beneath the black waters had left an indelible mark upon her psyche. Even now, she fancied that she could hear the distant lapping of the water at the castle walls, far below. She tried not to think of him, floating dead-eyed in the deep.

Mara attempted to distract herself from these unpleasant thoughts by counting her steps, a technique she had learned as a child who was prone to becoming lost in the forests surrounding her village. However, after three staircases and umpteen twists and turns in the corridors, she lost count. It was as though the attendant was taking a circuitous route to her lodgings on purpose – but if so, why? If his intent was to disorientate her, she had to concede that he had already more than succeeded. Yet, she would not allow him to see that concession within her – she simply would not show weakness. Whatever threat lay ahead, she must meet it with her back straight and her eyes wide open. Her father had taught her when to be stealthy and when to express dominance, both in the forests of her youth and in village life. The time for stealth would come – oh, she was sure of that – but now was an occasion demanding the latter.

Mara stuck her chin out as far as it would go, and rolled her shoulders back to increase her height to its maximum. She still had a child's stature next to Klove's giant henchman, but even such violent men as he were servile by nature. They rarely acted upon their own instincts, but rather the instincts of those who paid for their supper. Mara meant to capitalise on this. As the giant led her into a torchlit corridor, she spied an elegantly carved wooden door.

"Here," her guide announced in a voice as coarse as the flagstones upon which they had paused.

She slowed her pace as they approached, making the sweaty hulk wait. It seemed to work, as she detected a slight incline of his head, a slight bow in his upper body, as he pushed open the door.

What she had taken for reverence turned out to be a ruse when Mara took a tentative step into the room. The thug shoved her with such force that she was thrown onto the bed. She heard the door slam, the noise cutting off the curses that spilled from her mouth in her mother tongue. How dare he!

Mara picked herself up off the bed and marched over to the door. She twisted the ornate handle, expecting the door to be locked, but it opened. She looked outside for the henchman, intent on giving him a dressing down, but saw only a glimpse of his shadow before it disappeared along the passageway. She felt vulnerable, alone in the chill of the corridor, and decided to retreat into her room. It was, at least, warmer in there.

Her eyes narrowed slightly at the glow of lit candles. There was a subtle, and warming, scent of spice to the room. The wind whistled its lullaby around the castle's fortifications. An arched window framed the night sky, the moonlight glimmering on mountain crags and the swaying tips of emaciated fir trees that clung to them as if in desperation. She had known that state of being all too well. The winters when food was scarce for her family while others more fortunate grew fat on the other side of the valley, oblivious to the plight of their neighbours. The long nights listening to the low rumble of her father's voice, placating her distraught mother as she sobbed for lack of sustenance for her children. Again, Mara heard a wolf's howl but this time she did not flinch. She felt something approaching kinship with the beast. Perhaps it too was crying for lack of food for its children, alone in the hunt on a freezing mountainside. Stark desperation seemed to be currency in these climes.

And yet, glancing around her boudoir, there was such opulence behind these castle walls. Everywhere she looked she witnessed riches – in the elegant weave of the drapes, the polished surface of the dressing table – and she had an overwhelming feeling of being at home amidst them. At peace in a sense of belonging. It was as though this castle had whispered its call to her in a dream, and here she was heeding that call, welcoming its mysteries because she knew that at its heart this place offered riches as yet unrevealed.

Despite all of this, a shadow and a threat encircled her. A bitter aftertaste to all of the glamour and gold. Had not Klove's men already killed one of their number? And what was it he had said? Only one of them may leave? Mara's sense of belonging was quickly becoming usurped by one of dread.

She blinked rapidly, as though awakening from sleep, and saw her lodgings anew through unblinkered eyes. The opulence seemed crass to her now. The security and indulgence this place offered was a veneer. Thick castle walls were designed to keep the starving at bay, and food safely hoarded inside. She had to keep her wits about her as she had always done. A soft heart is vulnerable to thorns, as the saying went among her people.

Something flickered in the moonlight and Mara felt a pang of terror at her breast. She was being watched. A huge, black bat hung inverted in the arch of the window, its eyes reflecting dark red in the candlelight from the room. Mara saw the flash of white of its sharp incisors.

"Away, vermin!" she intoned, trying to sound brave but hearing the tell-tale vulnerability in her voice.

She rushed over to the window to startle the nocturnal beast, but it remained there, hanging, a silent observer. Mara reached for the curtains, reassured by their weight in her hands, and pulled them shut in one swift movement. She heard the unmistakable flapping of the bat's wings as it flew away into the night. Retreating to the bed and feeling a sudden chill, she climbed up onto it and then drew the covers around her body. The pillows were huge and soft, and smelled of the delicious spice that permeated the atmosphere of the room.

Strange. She had not noticed it before but there was a paper scroll on the bedside table, beside the candlestick. Mara thought the wax had dripped onto the envelope from the red candles above, but then realised that it bore a wax seal. She examined it and saw the shape of a dragon in the seal. The scroll carried no other markings. Curiosity at its peak now, Mara snapped the seal and opened it. Written in spidery handwriting, it read –

"You ... I know what you have done. Tonight, a reckoning is at hand. Know that only one shall leave this place.

For the others, damnation awaits. Should you slay a fellow guest, bring proof to my tower and you shall be rewarded. If you choose a coward's path then pray to whatever gods you worship, but know they will not save you. For I hold dominion in this cursed place and your fate is all but sealed.

Your friend, D."

Mara shuddered at the dread meaning of the words. Who on earth was "D"? And did they truly mean for honoured guests to slay one another like gladiators in an arena? Whatever game she had stumbled across here was a cryptic one indeed. Cryptic and macabre.

Glancing nervously at the bedroom door, Mara had a strong instinct to lock it, but alas, there was no key. She looked again at the scroll of paper, and then something else caught her attention, protruding from beneath the thick mattress. It was the spine of an old book. Her imagination fizzed as she imagined those who might have slept in this room before her. Had they too become players in some infernal and murderous game?

She prised the book from its hiding place and found that it was battered and torn. Turning the tome over in her fingers, she was disturbed to see that it looked as though it had been ripped from – or by – the jaws of some ferocious beast. She opened it all the same, and found that it was a diary or journal of some kind. Broken fragments of text revealed a fractured expedition of some kind across the Carpathian Mountains. Some pages contained tantalising puzzle pieces of maps, sketches and itineraries, while others had been torn away from the diary completely.

Mara turned the final page and found something tucked inside, perhaps as a bookmark. It was a scrap of parchment, older and softer to the touch than the pages of the book. She unfolded it and saw that it was a partial map of some kind. Her eyes traversed the corridors and hallways depicted there and she noticed that some areas of the map bore annotations. *The Great Hall.* Could that be the same place in which she and her travelling companions had witnessed the murder of poor, defiant Rasputin? Her heart skipped a beat when she saw the word "moat" scrawled beside the large oblong representing the hall. She traced the corridors depicted on the map with the tip of her index finger and found only two further legible landmarks. *The Courtyard,* read one and, *Trophy Room,* another. Someone had inscribed a crude cruciform shape beside the trophy room. The symbol spoke of sanctuary to Mara. Perhaps whichever human hand had drawn it had meant for someone to find it and to find some kind of safety or solace there.

Mara pursed her lips, remembering the ominous instruction in the note that had been left for her. *Only one shall leave this place.* She felt unsafe within the confines of her boudoir and vowed to remain alert, to survive this night as she had survived so many others when darkness had enfolded her in its cold embrace.

Tucking the map fragment back inside the book, she gathered her wits about her and prepared herself for whatever this night might bring.

CHAPTER EIGHT

Grayson had finished drinking his port before his guide had led him along the full length of one corridor.

This castle was bloody enormous, its size making it all the more eerie when travelling with some silent brute whose friend had just hurled a chap to his untimely death. His protestations that he should be stationed near to the ravishing young fortune teller's quarters had fallen on deaf – or, at the very least disinterested – ears, for his silent guide seemed intent on delivering him to the furthest and most remote part of the castle. Not to mention the coldest. Grayson had never liked the cold, his primary reason for taking a nip or three of brandy, and now that he was out of liquor his bones were beginning to feel the penetrating damp and cold of the castle's draughty corridors. And then there had been all that funny business with the moat, and that queer butler slurring cryptic warnings at them in the guise of some oddball parlour game. He should be making merry with that saucy wench in a cosy boudoir, not being led a merry dance by this homicidal village idiot!

Grayson pondered the course of action that had brought him to this sorry state of affairs. It was a rare moment of reflection, he knew, and he only wished he had some plucky young private to take dictation from him for his future memoirs. Oh, but Grayson had had no choice but to leave England, what with the accusations mounting against him, refute them though he may. He knew from his soldiering days that the East was a good corner of the map in which to lose oneself – not to mention give others the slip. It had worked well for him so far. He had dined out on his old war stories with anyone who had been willing to listen and to honour the bill. Yes, he had batted a good average to date, his trajectory East mapped by a trail of cleaned plates and soiled napkins in hostelries of every permutation imaginable.

And now here he was, in the arse-end of nowhere with a murderous thug as his guide. Grayson's gaze alighted nervously upon the dagger hanging from the thug's belt. He felt a rush of bile at his throat as fear gripped him harder than it had on any battlefield. Did that cad Klove mean for this ruffian to do away with him? Why else lead him this far into the castle and away from the last remnants of polite society? Grayson swallowed the bitter taste of his fear and slowed his steps a little. Put some distance between him and the brute, that would give him fair warning at least. But no warning came. The thug stopped dead in his tracks and Grayson let out an involuntary yelp, recoiling in such a state of shock and terror that he collided with the wall. He held up his hands in panicked surrender but with the wall behind him and the thug blocking the corridor, he had no escape route.

The brute regarded him with no discernible emotion in his eyes, which of course could be a very bad thing as well as potentially good. Grayson huffed and puffed, wiping cold sweat from his brow with the cuff of his jacket. The huge man reached out and Grayson clenched his eyelids shut in terror, waiting for the killing blow. For a moment he was frozen in time. The wall at his back was reminiscent of a boulder he had hidden behind for a spell during the Crimean. He had avoided death's kiss on that day and Grayson wondered if he really had used up all of his luck back then. Battlefield echoes of rifle balls whizzing by and the agonised screams of men he had known haunted him with their eerie refrains. He heard the brute in the passageway grunt. Felt the man's massive fist close around his cravat. Yes, the fiend meant to finish him, and Grayson was powerless to resist.

But he heard only a click. Then the brute dragged him sideways before shoving him back violently. Grayson expected to hit the wall but tumbled over and landed painfully on his backside.

Grayson opened his watery eyes. The thug had tossed him into a bedroom. In the gloom of the passageway he had failed to see the door, set into the wall beside him. Warm, inviting candlelight spilled over the flagstones onto which he had been flung.

"Your room," the behemoth said, and then slammed and locked the door.

Grayson heard him sauntering away down the passageway in the direction from which they had travelled. To add insult to injury, the bounder was whistling as he went. Actually whistling!

Grayson scrambled to his feet. "I say!" he called out in protest, "you can't just leave me here without anything to drink!"

He drummed his fists against the door but in truth, he was greatly relieved to see the back of Klove's sinister henchman. He'd had his chance to do away with him and had done no such thing, which meant that Klove wanted him alive.

The game was afoot, then. He would bide his time in the safety of this room and then decide what to do. Still trembling, he stood at the locked door listening to the diminishing footfalls of his burly guide until they were gone.

But then a new panic clawed at his heart. What if he wasn't safe here? What if he wasn't even alone in this room after all? What if he had been delivered unto his sticky end? Grayson would have to turn and face whatever peril lay in wait for him. He decided to count to ten silently before turning round, a trick he had learned when attempting to look brave and impressive on the battlefield – before legging it unnoticed to a safe hiding place as soon as the skirmish started. There had been many others like the Crimean boulder.

Ten ... Nine ... He controlled his breathing.

There is no one else in the room, he told himself, *you are safely alone here.*

Eight ... Seven ...

The sudden sputter of a candle dripping wax was all too much for him!

He wheeled around, eyes wide and mouth agape, and looked.

The sight before him exploded the tension in the manner of a pin pricking a balloon. All of the panic fell away from him in an instant and he laughed. How he laughed! The great bellowing laughter of a man who had received his pardon at the gallows came thundering out of him, filling every corner of the room with joy.

Grayson crossed to the table and, ignoring a scroll of paper that had been left there for him, picked up the silver hip flask that stood beside it. The hip flask was of the finest quality and beautifully engraved with a hunting scene that depicted a great stag, speared by huntsmen in the woods. Grayson's magpie mind was already making calculations as to what he might get for it from a pawnbroker at his next port of call. But the richest pickings, he hoped, lay within. He unscrewed the cap and sniffed at the hip flask's contents. Brandy, and the finest if the bouquet was anything to go on. And go on he most certainly would.

Raising the flask in a toast to imaginary convivialists, he exclaimed, "Here's to survival!" and, "Here's to bally beautiful old Blighty!" and finally, "God Save the Queen!"

Then he drank with enough gusto to better his toasts, before scooping up the scroll and staggering over to the bed. It was sealed with a rather ostentatious wax seal. Perhaps the dinner menu, he pondered hopefully.

He would read it in a little while, once he had slaked his thirst and rested his now-spinning head upon the plump pillows. By his third draught Grayson's limbs had become almost as liquid as the brandy and he began to drift into an intoxicated slumber.

***

A rattling at the door roused him from his brandy-induced sleep. Opening first one eye and then the other, Grayson sat up in bed. Knocking made him yelp in fright and he knocked the hip flask to the floor in alarm, along with the forgotten scroll of paper. No matter, he had drained the hip flask's contents anyway, but who was knocking? And more importantly, did they mean to murder him?

"H-hello?" he ventured, to no reply.

The lock clicked loudly. Perhaps Klove's brute had returned to finish him off. Ye gads, but his head was pounding, as though someone had taken an anvil to it. Had some monster poisoned his brandy? Seeing the door handle turn slowly, he felt the overwhelming urge to urinate. Holding onto his wits, and his bladder, Grayson ducked down behind the bed, putting it between him and door. The bed was no boulder, but it would bally well have to suffice!

Peering over the top of the bedclothes, he watched in anxious agony as the door handle continued turning. Then, the door creaked open. Grayson let out a little whimper – he couldn't help it – and retreated further behind the bed. If only he'd had the presence of mind to pick up the heavy candlestick that stood just feet away on the occasional table where he had found the hip flask.

If only.

Grayson's heart beat a wild tattoo in his chest as he waited for the brute's footsteps to enter the room.

Nothing. Not a sound.

Grayson risked a peep over the unkempt parapet of his bed. No one there.

But someone had unlocked the door.

The urge to relieve himself was all too great now and luckily, he found a chamber pot lying beneath the bed. He remained kneeling down and damn near filled it to the brim. Sighing with relief, he felt a shiver pass through him as the last drops left his bladder. He kept a weather eye on the door and considered his options. He surmised that two were available to him – he could wait for someone to come and discover him there or he could venture out and find a better defensive position – somewhere with more than one exit perhaps. He licked his dry lips and made up his mind.

Grayson was already some distance into the corridor when he realised he had neglected to bring the scroll of paper with him. Perhaps the note held some as-yet undetected clues. He was about to turn back to retrieve it when he saw a shadow pass over the wall of the corridor. Klove's henchmen, prowling the castle? What foul game were these ruffians playing at? Grayson looked around, frantic, and discovered an alcove housing a suit of armour. There was just enough room for him to hide behind the metal mannequin in the shadows, though he had to suck his belly in to do so without pushing the thing over. Too much plum pudding, if such a thing was possible. Grayson held his breath and watched as the shadow moved across the wall, shrinking until its owner was revealed.

Grayson watched from the alcove as the American walked over to the door of Grayson's former quarters. The fellow listened at the door, his face obscured by the brim of his large hat. After a few moments, he opened the bedroom door and went inside. Grayson was considering making a run for it when the chap quickly emerged from the room again. The American was holding the now unsealed scroll in his hand, which he then crushed in his big fist before sniffing at the air in the corridor like some horrid hybrid of man and beast. Grayson pressed his back right up against the alcove wall, hoping he would remain unseen. He held his breath in the quiet of the corridor and only released it when he heard the American sauntering away.

Grayson risked a quick look over the shoulder of the suit of armour. Yes, the fellow was going back the way he had come. What a relief! Grayson detected something in the way the man walked. Yes, that was it. It was as though the American owned the place, or at the very least, knew it well. This revelation did nothing to calm Grayson's nerves and he remained hidden for several minutes until he felt sure the chap had gone away. Then, just as he was about to steal out from his hiding place, Grayson saw someone else shuffling along the corridor.

It was the queer fellow from luncheon, and he looked more crazed than before, his eyes darting around as though reading hidden meanings in the castle's shadows. Grayson ducked back to remain out of sight of the strange man's searching eyes. The man shuffled closer and then something on the floor seemed to catch his attention. Grayson observed the man reach down and pick up the object, all the while glancing nervously around and along the corridor. It was the crumpled paper the American had tossed aside. The wild-eyed man held the paper up to the torchlight to better read its contents. Grayson watched as a tortured expression tangled the man's features into anger. He tore the note to shreds and stalked away down the corridor.

Grayson waited until the man was gone before emerging from his hiding place. He walked over to the jumble of torn paper and tried to reassemble it into some semblance of meaning but the task was beyond him. What vital knowledge eluded him?

He again considered the options available to him. Ever the survivor! Perhaps an alliance would work in his favour … but with whom? The American looked as though he'd be handy in a ruck, but he didn't trust that ruffian, not one iota. The high-collared chappie with the topper looked even less trustworthy. Bounder wouldn't even give his name! The stranger had exhibited a lack of decorum so much more extreme than even his own, that Grayson knew he could never be trusted.

The only remaining potential brother-at-arms was that queer fellow who had just torn the scroll into shreds. Alas, Grayson mused, he appeared to be stark staring mad. While that sort of carry on might do in a tight spot on the battlefield it most certainly would not do when one was in fear for one's own life. What about the elderly aristocrat? The Lady Sophia could as much as kill with a look, or one of her barbs, but she was also far too old and frail to keep up with someone as virile as himself.

Which left only one of their travelling party.

Mara, the fine young fortune teller. Yes, all roads led back to her. And the more he thought about it, the more it made sense. Despite her bravura exterior, he sensed that she was something of a lost soul. If he could find a chink in her armour – and he was, after all, an expert in that – he could sweep her off her feet. Yes, a union with her would be ideal, in all senses of the word! He felt positively revitalised at the thought of her sublime company, the thrill of the chase leading him quick march along the passageway.

CHAPTER NINE

The nameless wanderer struggled on, his heartbeat pounding in his ears, the walls of the castle seeming to mock him at every turn. The building's labyrinth mirrored that of his mind – ever darkening with doubt, and no sign of hope nor escape from its inevitable and inward spiral.

He ran until he could not run any longer. He walked, the soles of his feet burning with pain. He crawled until his knees began to bleed beneath his robes.

His energy now depleted, the nameless wanderer leaned back against the wall of the passageway, his skin slick with cold sweat and the tribal beat of his aching heart pounding ever louder in his ears.

Pulling his legs up and folding his arms around them, he wept silent tears, for he knew not what else to do. If only he could remember his name, his birthplace, or anything at all.

Then, he felt something within the folds of his robes, close to his chest, something that in his flight he had not noticed before. Retrieving the object from a pocket that had been sewn deep beneath the layers of cloth, he saw that it was a small book, bound in fine, brown leather.

Curious.

The book displayed no identifying marks, save for the myriad scuffs and indentations that suggested it was extremely old. He opened the book and flicked through its pages. Odd symbols and indecipherable text passed before his eyes like all the constellations in the heavens swirling overhead in a single night. Was it some kind of holy book, and was he a holy man to be carrying it? The book seemed to have some deeper meaning to him, but anything more than this vague fact lay beyond the grasp of his already clouded mind.

Sighing in frustration, he placed the book back inside its hidden pocket. He then studied the rings on his fingers, attempting to find meaning in these garish trinkets with their colourful stones, yet their meaning remained as insubstantial as a rainbow after the rain. Did the presence of such jewellery perhaps mark him as a merchant of some kind? His mind once more blank, he did at least notice one thing. One of the rings was plainer than the rest. Cast in white gold, it sat snugly on his wedding finger. Was he married? It was an intriguing thought indeed, that he may yet have a wife somewhere in the world. Was someone out there, wondering where her husband had gone?

Tears clouded his eyes and his mind flashed with sudden and vivid bursts of memory. Hot, summer skies from days past. Ziggurats towering over a bazaar that bustled with crowds of people. He glimpsed the beautiful face of a woman, his mind seizing upon her hazel eyes as though discovering jewels hidden in the sands of time. He felt himself reaching out to save her from shadows yet to fall. Were such feelings a kind of muscle memory? Or were they merely wishful thinking, fantasies to give him a sense of self, a story to call his own?

Yet one thing felt like a certainty to him: those eyes were achingly familiar. How he wished he could put a name to the woman's angelic face! The more he tried, the more she faded from view. It was as though her features were falling away from him, becoming as indistinct as grains of sand in an hourglass. The half-glimpsed memories receded just as quickly as they had arrived, and only an aching bitterness remained.

Then, he saw a flicker of light move across the wall at the end of the corridor. He wiped the tears from his eyes and clambered to his feet. Following the flickering light, he rounded a corner and, seeing the huge shadow of a man in the torchlight, skidded to a fearful halt.

Backing up round the corner, he peered out from behind the stonework to see the man was facing the wall, holding a flaming torch in one hand and studying the brickwork from beneath the brim of his hat.

There was something meticulous, rehearsed even, about the way the man ran the fingertips of his free hand across the stone. It was as though he was seeking some answer to an arcane question in the bricks and the mortar.

Within seconds, the giant had apparently found it, for a subtle click resounded in the tight confines of the passageway. The man put his sizeable shoulder to the brickwork and pushed, hard. A low rumble resonated from some hidden mechanism within and, to the wanderer's astonishment, the passageway wall opened inward to reveal a hitherto concealed entrance. As though sensing he was being watched, the huge man turned on his heel, waving the fiery torch in the wanderer's direction and startling him into ducking back round the corner in an instant.

Desperate moments passed as the nameless wanderer watched torchlight spill across the floor, and he expected to hear footsteps and to see the threatening shadow of the giant any moment.

Presently, the light dwindled and, hearing the low rumble again followed by the scraping of stone against stone, curiosity compelled the wanderer around the corner and into the passageway.

He reached the opening a fraction too late and when it closed, save for the dust it had kicked up from the floor, there was no sign there had been a door there at all.

Incredible.

The wanderer tried pushing his shoulder against the wall as his predecessor had, but it was no use. Where a secret passageway had opened up for the giant, there remained only solid, unyielding wall for him. Setting off again along the passageway he felt more nervous than ever about the imperceptibility of his surroundings. Could there be more hidden passageways in the walls that seemed once more to be closing in around him? Were others watching and waiting there, ready to pounce? The wanderer's eyes searched the shadows, finding only more sources of paranoia within them. And then his foot brushed against something soft and he stopped dead in his tracks.

He stooped to pick it up and found that it was a scroll of paper, just like the one he had found in the bedroom. He held it up to the torchlight and willed himself to be able to understand the meaning behind the indecipherable ink scrawls.

Why could he not understand?

Who *was* he?

Puzzles within puzzles, riddles within riddles, secrets wrapped in secrets – he could bear it no longer!

He tore the paper apart in fury at his predicament. Tossing the fragments aside, he watched them flutter to the dirty, stone floor. Despair overwhelmed him as he looked upon the ragged jigsaw of paper at his feet. Each torn piece mirrored the fractured and unsolvable puzzle of his mind.

CHAPTER TEN

L ady Sophia held a hand around the tallow candle to
protect it from the draught that threatened to extinguish
it utterly.

She held her breath as it flickered, hot wax trickling
and pooling inside the chipped porcelain bowl, and only
breathed out again when she had safely passed the window.
Shadows danced across the uneven stone wall as the candle
flame sputtered with renewed vigour and, for one terrifying
moment, she thought that someone was advancing upon her in
the corridor. Fear drove her back against the wall, her breath
caught in her throat, until she realised that naught but a shadow
was chasing her.

She reached for her locket again, a reflex action
whenever she was in distress, and realised that she was
panting. The onset of a fit of panic was the last ailment she
required at this present juncture and she silently told herself to
get a grip and soldier on. Popping open the locket, she held the

candle aloft so that she could see his face. So noble. So handsome. Well bred. Not like the riff-raff in this hellish backwater, no. Her Archibald had come from a noble line, his grandfather an explorer of some acclaim, his father the owner of a sizeable railway company, and he himself put in charge of overseeing construction of a new freight line that now carried tea and other goods across the Empire. That had been a proud day, when he had received his father's commission. Moving the candle closer, she saw beyond the little oval photograph and into the vision of memory, which danced golden as the flame she held in her hand. The flame which she carried within her soul for him, she would carry always. Her Archibald. She had endured a thousand living deaths since losing him, one for each time her heart had broken at the very thought of him.

Lady Sophia felt that all-too-familiar yearning in the pit of her stomach as her memory reached across the years in an attempt to find him. To locate the sunshine of his smile, and the rich timbre of his voice. But they had already began to elude her.

It was the trip to India that had caused the unravelling of the life they had carefully constructed together. He had always had such a strong constitution, Archibald. She supposed it was the dreadful hygiene in India that had upset his equilibrium so. She had known matters had taken a turn when his letters arrived less frequently, and then stopped. Archibald's father, whom she suspected had never really liked her, had been quick to dismiss her concerns.

"He's fine, my dear, just busy, very busy, you'll see."

But her father-in-law had always worked Archibald harder than the rest, she suspected to disprove favouritism to his board. And she knew now that this tendency did not help her husband's health. Not one bit. He had returned to England a changed man. His head hung low whereas previously he had always held it high. His once-bright voice and demeanour had been denigrated to mumbles and moans and, worst of all, he had not the strength to walk the hounds in the grounds as he had used to. Her staff had to wheel him out for his daily constitutional in a wicker bath chair. The shame. And the dogs barked incessantly and growled at him, as though smelling the illness that polluted his blood. Sophia winced as she heard an echo of his rattling breath. Her brow furrowed and a tear formed in the corner of one eye as she smelled the whiff of death in that room. In his final days, Archibald no longer wished to be out of doors in his chair. He lay in bed instead, hiding behind thick curtains that allowed no light into the room. Sophia allowed the tear to trickle down her face, feeling it turn cold as her grief began to turn to anger. Anger at the maidservant who was supposed to be nursing her poor dear husband on the night he—

What was that?

Sophia heard what sounded like a footfall coming from the corridor behind her. She had been walking all this time and not looking where she was going. Oh dear, now she truly was lost. Cold fear began to envelop her in its chill embrace. What might her Archibald do if he were here now, her poor dear husband? Why, he would take charge as he always did. Before India. Before he became a hollowed-out shell of the man she adored. She looked once more at Archibald's handsome face, before snapping the locket shut.

"I say, who's there?" She attempted to make it sound more like a command than a question, but there was no hiding the terror in her voice.

All had fallen silent.

Lady Sophia turned and proceeded in the direction she had been travelling prior to hearing the noise. The candle sputtered and the flame flickered wildly, threatening to leave her stranded in the darkness. Something wriggled past her foot and she cried out in alarm, almost dropping the candle, bowl and all, to the floor. The something screeched, a heart-piercing, otherworldly sound, and she glanced down to see that it was a large black rat. Shuddering, she headed away from the foul creature and up a short flight of steps that left her breathless once more when she reached their summit.

Catching her breath, she found herself in a small, narrow corridor, her feelings of unease dispelled somewhat by the sight of a wooden door up ahead. To her great relief, she noticed that it was a door of higher quality than the one which had led to the servant's quarters. The door was decorated with iron studs, and the handle looked rather ornate. This was much more like it. She turned the handle and pushed, and the door swung open.

Lady Sophia let out a sigh at what she saw. Not her usual dismissive sigh but rather a great expression of relief. The large boudoir was exquisitely furnished, and decorated with beautifully woven wall hangings that made the room feel immediately warm to her as she stepped inside. The desired four-poster bed dominated the room, its frame leafed with gold and elegant drapes cascading down like a silken river. An enormous bearskin rug lined the floor beside the bed, the glass eyes of the beast reflecting the light of the candles that filled the room with yet more inviting warmth.

She closed the door behind her and quickly located the key, turning it in its lock and feeling safer upon hearing the satisfying click that it made as she did so. She discarded the peasant's tallow candle, placing the chipped bowl on a marble-topped dresser.

Why, this room could rival even that of the master bedroom at my own estate, she thought.

Every creature comfort seemed to be present in this space, surely the best-kept secret in the entire castle. Her strategy to locate a luxurious hideout had paid off, with dividends. A crystal decanter filled to the brim with strange green liquor, perhaps absinthe, gleamed atop a silver tray beside two crystal goblets. A perfume diffuser sat beneath an ornately framed mirror, its bulb decorated in the finest gold brocade. Beside the huge recessed window, a reading chair with footstool looked most inviting. Lady Sophia was about to kick off her shoes to relieve her aching, swollen feet, when she glimpsed movement at the corner of the room. For a horrible moment she thought someone was standing there – and had been standing watching her all along – when she realised it was just a painting. The frame trembled slightly, disturbed by a chill breeze that was making the drapes seem to come alive around her.

She picked up a fresh candle in a silver candlestick and crossed to the painting to take a closer look. The drapes of the four-poster bed rose and fell as she passed them, as though borne on some unseen, insidious breath. Reaching the painting, she saw that the figure depicted there wore a high hat, his beard and whiskers long and jet-black. The pallor of his skin marked him as a native to these parts and his eyes – those eyes – seemed to see beyond the confines of oil, canvas, and frame, piercing her with their sharp, intelligent gaze. She had never before seen a visage that looked so old, and yet so young and vital all at once. The effect of the painting was quite unsettling and she looked away from it. The candle flickered slightly and she discerned something in the wall beside the painting. The brickwork there had been laid differently to the surrounding wall and, as she peered closer, she saw a distinct, dark line that disappeared behind one of the wall hangings. The hanging, too, was undulating in the same cold breeze that had disturbed the painting, and she pulled it back slightly to reveal the shape of a door, concealed in the stone.

Gooseflesh prickled her neck and back as she heard a clicking sound behind her. She whirled around and saw the door handle to the room turning slowly. The key remained in the lock. She was about to cross the room to pluck the key from the locked door when the handle turned again from side to side in dreadful and violent motions. Someone was determined to get in! Remembering the chilling words in the scroll from the servant's bedroom, Lady Sophia turned back to the secret door. She reached out with one trembling hand, the other still clutching the candlestick, and pushed gingerly against the door in the wall. To her surprise, she heard a faint click and the secret door swung open. Strands of cobweb stretched to breaking point across the opening as though clinging to the secret beyond. The cool breeze rose in intensity and with it, the most intoxicating scents of cooking wafted into the room like a balm. A sharp series of knocks and bangs from the main door startled her. It sounded like whoever wanted to enter was attempting brute force. Whomever it was surely meant to do her harm. What had the note said? "If you slay one of the others ..." Sophia's rising terror at this new threat took her a few steps forward, through the opening afforded by the secret door and into a passageway beyond. It was long and narrow but also felt dusty and dry, as though it had remained hidden for ages. The knocking and banging behind her intensified.

Sophia took another step forward and heard the scraping of stone against stone as the secret door slid shut again behind her. She cried out in surprise, her voice echoing into silence down the passageway.

She pushed against the door to make sure her intruder could not follow. Pushing against the door did no good, it stood as firm as the wall that flanked it. At least she was safe on this side of the secret door, but she could not linger, for fear that her would-be murderer might find it too.

Taking a breath for courage, Lady Sophia held her candle aloft and set off along the passage, brushing aside dusty cobwebs as she went. All the while she felt thankful that she had neglected to kick off her shoes in the bedroom. Her superior instincts had guided her to the opulent boudoir, but would have meant nothing if she had fallen asleep in that inviting four-poster bed before the intruder came creeping to her door. Fortune, and her keen senses, had guided her to the secret door, and now she must invent a new plan.

As she progressed along the hidden passageway, those sharp senses of hers detected distant, aromatic scents of roasting meats and baking pastry. She began to salivate within an instant and the delicious cooking smells seemed to urge her on.

CHAPTER ELEVEN

I follow the sounds of their voices and footfalls deeper into the depths of the castle.

It is cooler down here and I am glad of my greatcoat, which goes some way to protect me from the Carpathian chill. It has withstood many a freezing London fog in its time, and serves me well once more. Hearing footsteps doubling back toward me, I tighten my grip around the handle of the assassin's blade. Then, there is silence. Strange. I peer from the shadows and see a lone shadow cast by the flickering torchlight: Klove. He has left her alone! Oh, but this is too deliciously perfect. All things toward their end. I proceed at haste until I find the open door to some shabby old servant's quarters. Candlelight flickers in the far distance and I put two and two together. Klove abandoned the old bint down here but she's only gone and wandered off in search of something better! The old cow has a head start. The thrill of the chase and all that.

My achievements thus far have been most illuminating. I am almost embarrassed to think back to how I used to rush so, in the early stages of my career. The last one in particular, before I had to hop off the island so plod could chase his tail, was as slow as I could have hoped. Slower, even. I recall the deft hand with which I worked the knife, and close my eyes for a moment, seeing red atop the bedside table. I risk a sigh, to siphon off the anticipatory tension that always comes before another kill. My sharp ears pick out the distant, muffled sound of Lady Sophia's footfalls as she wanders the corridors, alone. I breathe deeply, but quietly, and then set off after her.

I can smell the lavender and talcum powder scents of her eau de parfum. It is an alien smell amidst the honest dank and murk of the castle, the stone of which seems to drip perspiration as though it is a living organism. Lady Sophia's trajectory takes us up stairs and across an enclosed walkway into the heart of the castle. True to form, she appears to be seeking out higher-class lodgings. Good. The deeper we go into this vast building, the less likely it will be that anyone will hear her scream. And then the blade and I can take our sweet time with her. I lick my lips, and my tongue brushes against the interior of my high collar. My mouth forms a grin as I think of the taste of her noble blood. And then I spit in recognition that it would taste exactly the same as the street women. Tainted with the same salt-pig ignorance. The same baseness. The low dark of their corrupt sex. The leather of my gloved hand stretches thin around the knife, I am so eager now to make the first cut.

Her scent grows stronger as I draw near. Her seventy-odd years on earth will soon come to an end and she will begin her true journey into enlightenment, liberated by the tip of my blade. My dark workings upon her flesh will release her into the hereafter, and she will know then that I have saved her, made her clean. I pause at the threshold into a closed passageway, and watch her look of delight as she opens the door. Her craggy face is bathed in the golden light of candles as she looks with wonder upon her sanctuary. It is a fitting venue indeed for a sow like this one, who considers herself "high born". She came into the world in a room like this, no doubt, spat from her mother's loins unto a world of privilege and luxury. And she will ascend in another room just like it. The blood and joy of her birth shall be bettered by the blood and terror of her departure, I'll see to that.

I watch her close the door, and wait, even though it is torturous to do so. I know the importance of patience, after all. All those nights spent watching, waiting, in the filth and the chaos of East End alleyways. Each and every one worth the brief moments of salvation I have been blessed to gift those street women. The looks in their piggy eyes as they see me for the first and last time! I lurch toward the door and have to force myself to stop, and to lean against the wall of the passageway, making believe it is just another alley, and reminding myself they are more compliant if I allow them to settle.

A rat scurries along where the wall meets the floor. Its red eyes glint as it passes me. I stamp down on its plump body with my heel and feel its bones crack under my weight. It squeals as I twist my foot around and finish it off. The internal logic of its organs becomes undone, rupturing and popping wetly beneath my shoe. I kick its limp body aside and then wipe the sole of my shoe against the flagstones.

Now, it is time.

I hold the blade ready and advance upon the door. With my free hand, I twist the door handle noiselessly. It is locked, of course, so I take out the note from my pocket and slide it under the door, directly below the keyhole. A few sharp shoulders to the door (the old bag will no doubt sleep through them anyway, and if not, how frightened will she be! How primed for my arrival!) and I hear the key drop to the floor. Sliding the paper, and with it the key, under the door, I pop the key in the lock, turn it, and then in one fluid motion, step into the room.

The warmth and glow from the candles hits me, but I am unperturbed. I look to the bed, certain she will be waiting for my sacrament there, but find that it is empty. I glance to the dresser, and the chair beside it is also unoccupied. Rage and bile boil in my chest and throat. I slash thin air with the blade that is now more eager than ever to taste a woman's flesh. Where has she gone? I search the room in a daze of numb rage, seeking some en-suite bathing room or hidden antechamber that simply is not there. On the rug beside the bed, I find a crumpled sheet of parchment. I stoop to pick it up and then carry it over to the dressing table where the light is better for reading.

I sit at the dresser and feel the stab of disgust at the sight of the feminine objects stationed there. With a swipe of my blade I knock the perfume diffuser to the floor, followed by the powder brush, and then the whole stinking lot of it, save for the oil lamp. Straightening out the paper to give clarity to the words written upon it, I hold it closer to the lamp so that I can read it. The note is a facsimile of the instruction that awaited me in my intended quarters. So the game is afoot for each of us. Easy for me to accept – welcome sport indeed, perhaps. But a frail old woman like Lady Sophia would no doubt be petrified. How has she managed to leave the room without me seeing her? I curse myself for waiting too long, this time. If only I had not dallied with the rat and missed my chance to put an end to bigger vermin. I screw up the paper and toss it onto the dresser.

And then, I inadvertently look into the mirror.
My flesh turns cold.
I recoil.

My reflection disorientates me. Or rather, reflections, because a kaleidoscope of fragmented features are reflected back to me. Angular sections of top hat frame distorted patches of skin. An eye here, a nose there, but none of them adding up to the entirety of a human face. The mirror is a swirling pool of eviscerated features, all of them my own, but none of them me. I wonder for a moment if the mirror is cracked, but in my dark heart I know that it is not so.

Rather, I am the one who is broken.

I wrench my gaze away from the mesmerising patchwork of the mirror, and find that I am being observed. A trio of women, so much quieter than me to enter unnoticed! Or perhaps it was the cursed mirror that distracted me. I show them the blade, turn its sharp edge to catch the candlelight. They don't even flinch, not a one of them. The wanton women even see fit to smile and laugh! Their eyes are unafraid, and their mannerisms completely unashamed, a disposition matched by their scanty garments. They bare their teeth in smiles both cruel and seductive. I look away, rage burning inside me at this intrusion.

Impossible.

The mirror shows no reflection of the women, even though they are standing in the room directly behind me!

I turn back to face them and find that they have each drawn nearer. My senses are filled with their combined scents – earth, rain, and fire – overwhelming me with olfactory intensity. I raise the blade to slash at these vile harridans of the night, to quash their scent with that of blood alone, but as I prepare to strike, the boldest of the three grasps my wrist in her hand and I am unable to move.

It is as though my flesh has turned to ice.

I hear the blade hit the floor, the sound fuzzy and distant. She pulls at my cuff, revealing the flesh of my wrist from beneath the lip of my glove. Her eyes widen hungrily at the sight of my veins. I feel my pulse betraying my mortality to her. I should murder her where she stands, release her dirty interior to the heavens, but I am powerless in her freezing grip. Her sisters close in either side of me. To my horror, I feel the collar of my greatcoat open and fall away from my face. Their freezing touch is anathema to my skin.

I am revealed.

It is unbearable, yet still I cannot move. I hear them singing, a sickly-sweet sonorous melody that makes me want to vomit. I feel hot breath against my wrist, my face, my neck. The scents of sweet chocolate and rancid meat overpower me. I am undone. They hiss in unified delight, and then bare their sharp teeth. My hand reaches for the absent blade. I see red.

And then I see no more as I spiral into blackness.

CHAPTER TWELVE

Grayson's legs and feet ached from walking the castle halls.

His eyes had grown weary from exposure to so much darkness. Each passageway looked much the same as the next and he had to admit he had become woefully lost in their maze. Making an about-face like a private on parade, he attempted to retrace his steps, but this only exacerbated his lack of an internal compass. He felt sure he had passed this way before – perhaps even twice.

Grayson then decided upon a new tactic. He would take only left turns from now on, and if that failed to lead him anywhere useful he would try only right turns for a while. He proceeded with the renewed purpose of a man with a plan – however tenuous that plan might be – but soon enough, he recognised the same scalloped ceiling that he'd passed under just minutes ago.

To the right, quick march! Left, right, left, right ...

The imagined blare of his sergeant's voice urged him on in the other direction. The corridor widened, and Grayson felt a breath of cool air across his face. He continued, feeling the breath become a cool breeze. This was progress. As he followed the corridor its full length, Grayson felt a rush of elation to see a staircase he had not yet encountered branching off from the end of the corridor. Saints preserve him, his right turns might have actually worked! Grayson navigated his descent of the stairs as quickly as his aching limbs would allow, and found himself overlooking some kind of courtyard. He was on a balcony some fifty feet above.

Peering over the crenelated wall, he saw that the courtyard was overgrown with knotted vines that coiled around fallen masonry and tall statues that stood guard over the space from their plinths. A makeshift log store had been constructed in one far corner, its planks looking more weathered than the firewood they contained. Elsewhere, wooden walkways were lashed to the walls with thick rope, accessible only by the ladders that leaned against them from ground level. A fire flickered in a pit to one side of the courtyard, illuminating the wall nearest to it with its glow. At the far end of the balcony upon which he stood, Grayson saw the curved wall of a tower. There was an open doorway at its centre.

As he walked closer to it, he saw that the doorway led into a spiral stairwell which led down to the courtyard. He followed the steps down, taking care in the gloom, for this part of the castle was lit only by the fire in the courtyard via slim arrow slits built into the structure. The fire crackled like some primal language, drawing Grayson closer to its warmth, which he welcomed in the sudden chill of the night air. He looked aloft and saw great, thick clouds diffusing the moonlight. A veritable cauldron of a storm was bubbling overhead. He held out his hands to warm them and studied the castle walls in idle curiosity. How long had they stood there, cold and impenetrable?

The cold breeze intensified, jostling the flames of the firepit. In this changing light, Grayson spied details in the stonework he had not noticed before. Beneath the battlements, a series of pictographic carvings were inlaid into the stone. They were carved in a language he did not recognise, but which carried an atmosphere of evil, somehow. His eye began to pick out further details here and there – a skull, or rather a series of them, a lightning flash, and something that looked on first glance like a gallows. As the flames shifted again, the shape became clearer: it was an inverted cross. Grayson shivered at the sight of such blasphemy. He wasn't what you might call a dedicated churchgoer – far from it – but even so, he was all too aware of the transgression of such a symbol.

A shiver passed through his body.

The fire was now doing nothing to dispel the chill that had begun to gnaw at Grayson's bones. An icy blast of wind brought a new sensation to his ears. It was a sound, indistinct at first, but then growing louder, and clearer. Trickling water. His curiosity led him away from the fire and toward the source of the sound. What he had thought to be another of the old stone statues was, in fact, a fountain. The pillared structure was elegantly carved from black marble, which had veins of white and grey running through it. The clouds parted, allowing moonlight through, and revealing the fountain's finer details. Grayson stepped closer, studying the cherubic faces carved there. Some had metal pipes protruding from their mouths, through which dirty black water was trickling. The edges of the pipes had corroded, and glistened an eerie blue-green in the moonlight.

Grayson peered into the jet-black water, which cast no reflection. He reached for it with his fingertips on an impulse, and quickly retracted them upon another. Grayson could not look at the dark water without remembering the moat, and the Russian dragged under its surface. He could not look upon his own outstretched hand without seeing the afterimage of the dying man's, and how it had clawed at the air!

Willing these disturbing thoughts away, Grayson took to strolling around the perimeter of the fountain. He noticed, with further disquiet, that the carved marble faces grew progressively monstrous with each step he took. The final face in the sequence was bestial, with large fangs protruding over a painfully thin bottom lip. The artist had managed to create eyes that no matter from which angle Grayson viewed them, remained black in their sockets; a hue rivalled only in its depth of darkness by the fluid that trickled from between those savage-looking incisors. In an attempt to lighten his spirits Grayson tried to recall a village fountain upon which he had once seduced a milkmaid. This fountain was its antithesis, the black water spilling like bile as if from the very fount of all evil itself. He backed away, yearning now for the warmth of the fire. But then another sound froze him where he stood.

A low murmur, which sounded to Grayson like Hell clearing its throat, rumbled across the courtyard. All the hairs stood up on the back of his neck when he saw the source of the sound. A procession of black-robed figures was filing into the courtyard, the hems of their garb dragging on the ground. Their faces were hidden within the folds of black hoods. They could have been phantoms save for the noise they were making – or perhaps *because* of it. Each held a thick, black candle in their hands, and each continued the guttural drone of his fellows so that it became a defiled Gregorian chant without end. As they processed into the courtyard, they began to fan out into some kind of formation.

They were forming a circle – and Grayson was at its centre!

Caught in limbo between the fire and the fountain, Grayson's mouth twitched as he considered what to do next. He was in a fix and no mistake. Grayson kicked himself for descending the steps into this accursed courtyard. If he had remained aloft, he could have stolen away, unseen. He now had but moments until he would be encircled by those weird, throat-singing harbingers. Fear took hold of his limbs, his feet carrying him backwards until he collided with the marble lip of the fountain.

The fountain!

It was no Crimean boulder, no dugout or trench, but it would have to do. He dashed around to the shadowy side of the structure and, trying his best to ignore the sharp-fanged visage of the monstrous cherub spewing black water at him, ducked beneath its curved side. He was just silently congratulating himself on finding a pretty good hiding place when he realised his miscalculation. The hooded figures were forming a circle in the courtyard as predicted. But what he had failed to predict was that they were forming a circle around the fountain itself. He felt his stomach become a sinkhole of despair. He had inadvertently positioned himself at the very epicentre of some very queer occult goings-on! He shrank back into the shadows as far as he could. The lip of the fountain seemed to be concealing him thus far, but for how long? As the figures drew nearer, tightening their infernal circle, Grayson felt sure he would be discovered at any moment. His eyes alighted on the doorway to the stone tower, wherein the spiral stair lay.

It was less an act of bravery, and more one of desperate self-preservation that forced him from out of his hiding place. He crawled across the courtyard, trying not to cry out at the pain in his knees as sharp stone dug into them. All the while, the unholy droning of the hooded throng rose to a demonic, fever pitch. Their combined voices sounded like an army of savages baying for blood beneath the ritualistic dagger of moonlight that pierced the courtyard through the clouds. The very air in the courtyard felt heavy and condensed, somehow, as though it were laden with evil.

Grayson could see that he was mere yards away from the open doorway now. Escape was firmly within his crosshairs. Although spurred on by this newfound hope, he felt his chest tighten, his breathing becoming laboured. His heart throbbed in time with the evil droning of the occultists. He dared not look back to check if he had been seen. Almost there. He could see the first step of the spiral staircase within the tower. He stood up.

The black shape had outflanked him before he could even react to it. It appeared so suddenly and in such close proximity that it was as though night had fallen around his entire person. He felt a great hand fall upon his shoulder, heavy as a rock, seizing him. His knees buckled as he was forced down onto his knees. The door to the tower stairwell seemed leagues away, its refuge denied to him by this cruel and powerful hand of fate. He felt pressure at the back of his skull. Then came a sickening numbness. The blow to the back of his head had sent him spiralling into unconsciousness. The hellish chanting echoed a litany in his ears as he fell. Then came silence as his face hit the ground.

CHAPTER THIRTEEN

The ominous and all-pervasive feeling that she was being watched accompanied Mara's every step as though it were her shadow.

The dread import of the note that had been left in her boudoir had only added to her sense of desperation. Following the map fragment from the journal she had found beneath the bed had led her in ever decreasing circles. Holding her candle closer to the paper, she attempted to find her bearings, but every corridor looked as confusing on paper as it did in the castle. She was about to begin retracing her steps, when a sudden screech pierced the noiseless enclave of night.

Mara rushed over to an archway where the shutters were open to the night air. Looking about her, she caught sight of a bat, spiralling across the treetops below the castle battlements. Something flashed from those treetops, and Mara realised that she was making eye contact with one of night's denizens. The owl blinked, screeched again, and then soared majestically from its branch in silent pursuit of the bat that had flown by. The sounds were the very stuff of childhood memory for Mara. The ancient trees that encircled her tiny village had dwarfed it, and they too played host to all manner of creatures. She had observed their habits with such frequency that they became kin to her, and had schooled her in the primal knowledge that to hunt is to survive. Her father had told her stories of these beasts, some of which he christened with names, as she had lain on her straw mattress in their timber-framed cottage.

He drew inspiration for his stories from some behavioural tic or other he had witnessed while out setting traps in the forest, or while chopping wood at the perimeter of his work yard. It was through these tales that Mara had become able to make her peace with the wild world beyond her window. In time, she had learned to love all of God's creatures. Except perhaps the wolves that she and the other villagers feared.

Mara gazed at the swaying trees that blanketed the surrounding mountains in evergreen and wondered how many more pairs of glowing eyes were concealed within their shadows. She shivered at the cold breeze from the open archway and drew her shawl tighter around her. The sensation of the wool brushing against her skin reminded her of the woollen blanket she had snuggled beneath as a child. How she had cried when she had heard packs of wolves outside her bedroom window. Now she was grown, Mara understood that this had been her first inkling of her own physical vulnerability in the vastness of nature. She remembered one such night when her father had come to settle her down to sleep again, as he always did when she'd had nightmares.

"I'm afraid of the wolves, Dadda," she had said, hating how small her voice sounded in comparison to those howls in the night.

"This is their home too, my poppet. They have as much right to be here as we do. They are a family, just as we are. Leave them alone, and they'll ignore you," her father had advised.

The memory of his voice, its deep timbre, made Mara ache for a home that was now long gone.

"But what if they won't leave me alone?" she had asked, quite reasonably, she thought. Her father had just laughed and then ruffled her long hair. It had been his way of placating her, although it rarely worked because she would still lie awake long nights listening to the wolves howl.

Then the rich landowners had come, and everything had changed.

The mansion atop the hill had stood empty for several years after its owner, Baron Meinster, died of old age. His only heir was abroad, making his fortune in France, until rumours of war sent the heir back to the refuge of the family pile. The incumbent baron brought with him a wife and a young daughter, Carmella, who was Mara's age. The winter had been especially harsh that year and larders were running empty long before spring. The villagers, hearing that a new baron had been installed in the mansion, began the daily pilgrimage to the top of the hill, bearing trinkets and rustic wares that they hoped to exchange for food. But the young baron was something of a firebrand, and he ordered the starving villagers off his land and banished them from his property. All save one young woman.

Mara.

Her father had encouraged her to visit her fortune telling talents upon the landowners. She would have been turned away, too, had it not been for Carmella's insistence that she wished to have her fortune told. Not wishing to displease his only daughter, the baron allowed Mara to enter the mansion, where she received a sumptuous hot meal and a place near the fire in the palatial drawing room. Mara had never before witnessed such riches as those on display in the mansion. Crystal chandeliers twinkled in the candlelight. Gold-framed portraits of the baron's noble ancestors towered over her on papered walls that seemed so impossibly high to a girl who had grown up in a tiny cottage. And the jewel in this crown was surely Carmella. Her beauty was already the talk of the village, where it seemed everyone from the goatherd's son to the publican's bottle washer fancied themselves as potential suitors. But only Mara was allowed an audience with her.

She had felt nervous about telling the young woman's fortune. What if the cards described some ill omen or terrible portent? Mara felt her stomach churning as she flipped over the first card, and then relief to find that it was The Lovers. Carmella, it seemed, had an emerging interest in matters of the heart and, after that first reading, invited Mara back to read her fortune on a weekly basis. Mara never felt any more comfortable amidst such opulence but did the readings out of duty to her struggling father, who had come to rely upon the silver that crossed his daughter's palm and fell into his at the end of each week.

The wheel of the year turned to summer, and with it the social season for Mara's hosts. To Mara's surprise, and her father's delight, she received an invitation to Carmella's coming out ball. Carmella had her come up to the house and helped pick out one of her own elegant ballgowns for Mara to wear. She dismissed her maidservant, opting instead for she and Mara to style one another's hair. Carmella spoke of their friendship, and Mara found herself blushing to be on the receiving end of such affection from a woman of higher status. Perhaps worst of all, she began to enjoy it, and to crave it.

Mara had stepped onto the parquet floor of the mansion's ballroom feeling giddy as a child.

But then, the joy had been knocked out of her.

Carmella, it transpired, had only invited Mara so that she could perform party tricks for her. She read fortune after fortune at a little card table beside a draughty window, while all around her the guests drank and danced, and laughed. After they had imbibed yet more wine, they began laughing at her. Mara had to fight off the unwanted advances of several of the men who came to her table under the pretence of wishing to hear their fortunes. It was only when the son of a count – whom Mara knew Carmella had a thing for – approached her table that Mara saw her exit strategy. Drunken revellers gathered round to hear the young suitor's fortune, along with, of course, Carmella herself. Mara dramatized her reading in the hushed candle glow. She made sure that the fortune she read for the count's son spelled disaster for his pairing with her pay-mistress. The gathering erupted into joyous gossip and laughter, all of it at Carmella's expense.

Furious, Carmella had Mara thrown out of the mansion, but not before she had forced her to remove the ball gown in front of all her cackling guests.

"Look at the poor fortune teller," she had said, and laughed, their friendship very much at an end (if indeed it had really existed at all). *"She's skin and bone, not airs and graces. And dressed in rags! How dare she think she had a place among her betters, here, in society!"*

Cruelly humiliated, Mara had returned home to her father in tears. His fury at his daughter's ordeal was short-lived, and it soon transpired that he had priorities over and above his daughter's well-being.

"They did at least pay you?" he asked.

The look on his face when she fell silent filled Mara with dismay. That was all she was to him – an organ grinder's monkey forced to perform for whatever coins were tossed their way.

Morning came, and with it, grave news. The count's son had taken ill and died suddenly in the night. Carmella had taken to her room, and her doting father issued instruction that no one might disturb her.

Winter came around once more, and this time it was even harsher than the previous year's. The villagers were soon on their knees from hunger, and two of the elderly perished from the cold. They were forced to eat their animals, save for the poultry. And those, too, when the scrawny beasts were inevitably starving and unable to lay eggs. A delegation, led by Mara's father, went up to the mansion house to beg for food from the baron.

He would not even open the gates.

Dejected, the villagers returned to their hovels. Mara became frightened of the wolves once more, hearing in their howls how hungry they too had become. It was as though the creatures could smell the villagers' desperation. She knew it was only a matter of time before nature's order of things spelled ruin for them all. Mara thought of the mansion and its riches, her heart aching for the happier times when she and Carmella would sit beside that roaring fire. She thought of all the crystal, silver and gold that the baron had hoarded. Just a tiny fraction of it could save the lives of so many villagers.

Their ruin was all Carmella's fault. Her pride had cut off the only source of income left to Mara and her father, and now the very existence of Mara's people was under threat. She had to do something.

Mara had the ear of the entire village. Her art in telling fortunes meant every door, and every heart, lay open to her in her community. And so began her whispers and gentle asides. Carmella had brought witchcraft to the village. She had driven the count's son to suicide with a spell. Her lustful pride was so great that if she could not have him, then no one would. Her vile, black magic had brought the wrath of God upon them all.

There had to be balance in all things. Were they not being punished for Carmella's sins?

Within days, her whispers had become the angry protestations of an entire village. Up to the mansion they roared, bearing torches and with Mara's own father in their vanguard. They demanded audience with the baron and when he refused, they stormed the gates.

Mara had not intended for things to go quite so far.

The angry mob, driven mad with hunger, ransacked the mansion. They took all that they could, gorging themselves, stuffing their threadbare pockets and loading up their ramshackle carts until the wheels buckled. And, when the silver and gold had been plundered, and the pantries emptied, they turned their righteous rage elsewhere. To Carmella herself. They dragged her screaming from her room and outside into the freezing air. She had the feral look of a wild thing after all those weeks of grief-stricken solitude, her hair matted and her eyes twitching in dark sockets, swollen by tears.

"Witch!" they shouted, *"you are the source of all our ills! 'Tis your dark art and poison tongue that have laid waste to our crops. 'Tis our blood on your dainty little hands."*

"String her up," some said.

"Burn her," said others still, *"burn the witch!"*

"We must try her as a witch," Mara's father interjected. *"We must not become savage nor base as she is!"*

Mara knew in her heart that they already had. The mansion was ablaze. Windows shattered and drapes caught fire. The baron had fought against the mob, felling one villager, and had retreated inside. The crowd roared as the mansion roof caved in, the entire building now a conflagration of purifying flames. All those lofty portraits that had once looked down on her from their gilded frames melted into fuel for the fire. The Meinster bloodline was almost at an end as the mob watched it burn. And Mara saw the same cruel glee in her fellow villagers' eyes as she had seen in those of the gentry when they had humiliated her.

She had not meant for things to become quite as brutal as they did.

Yet they did, all the same.

Carmella tried to defend herself, even in the throes of her grief at the loss of her father and her home. She railed against the crowd, willing them to perceive her innocence and to acknowledge the true witch among them: Mara. This accusation tipped the mob into a frenzy and they restrained Carmella while others began building a funeral pyre. Mara's father defended Carmella then, urging his fellows to calm, but they instead turned against him.

"She's bewitched him!" they cried, *"she means to trick us. He'll have us test her witchcraft, only she'll use it to falsely prove herself innocent. Suffer not a witch to live!"*

Mara's father held firm, and she wondered if perhaps he felt guilt at how he had treated his daughter and so wanted to do better by Carmella. Maybe that was his way of making amends. Yet seeing her own father defend her false friend, who had brought so much humiliation, pain and conflict into her life and the lives of those closest to her, twisted in Mara's heart like a knife. Bitterness seeped into the wound in her heart and she stood silently by as the wrath of the village crashed down upon her father in an unstoppable torrent of violence.

When it was over, and his lifeless body lay still on the frozen ground, Mara saw the first torch lowered into the pyre. The villagers, now so innovative in their cruelty, added burning timbers from the mansion Carmella had called home to the very instrument of her immolation. As the flames took hold, Carmella's screams of anguish soon followed. Mara carried them with her as she stole away through the outermost reaches of the village and into the forest. She knew the wolves would be waiting for her there.

Let them come, she thought, gathering her shawl around her, *for I am now far too bitter a morsel for any beast to digest.*

Mara's bitter memories gave way to the import of the present. She blinked away cold tears and took a last look out across the treetops before turning her attention back to the castle passageway. Drawing her shawl tighter around her arms, which had begun to grow numb with cold, she moved on.

An open archway lay at the end of the passageway and, as she neared it, Mara was surprised to hear voices. She slowed her pace, approaching with a hunter's stealth, listening intently. The voices were many yet chanted as one, in some ancient tongue unknown to her young ears. As she crossed the threshold of the archway, the passage opened up onto a high balcony bordered by a balustrade of stone columns. Mara crept over to one of the pillars and, careful to remain in the shadows, peered out over the balcony's edge.

The scene below was one from a forgotten time. A circle of black-clad figures, their faces concealed beneath cowls, stood around a fountain that formed the courtyard's centrepiece. Mara quickly unfolded the map fragment she had discovered in her boudoir, and realised that she had discovered the first of its landmarks.

Sudden movement from behind the fountain drew her attention and she saw the Englishman from her travelling party sneaking away from the chanting figures as they assembled around the fountain. His clumsy crawling was the opposite of stealth and sure enough, she saw three of the figures peel away from the group in pursuit of the oblivious Englishman. Mara raised her hand to her mouth, biting down on her knuckles for fear of being detected. She watched in wide-eyed horror as the strange cultists seized the Englishman by the shoulders and forced him to the ground, before one of them delivered a blow to the back of his head with a cudgel.

Mara pressed her body against the column, anchoring herself to it as she watched the trio of hooded figures dragging the unconscious Englishman from the courtyard. As they disappeared from view, the chanting grew louder and it was as though the remaining worshippers – of what, she did not dare imagine – were compensating for the absence of three of their comrades.

The chanting reached fever pitch, each voice entwining with the next until it formed a shrill, never-ending wail. She pressed her hands to her ears against the unholy racket and was about to retreat from the balcony when she saw something astonishing.

The fountain, until now a mere trickle of dirty water, began to issue forth a gush of dark crimson blood that splashed over its marble edifice, staining the strange faces that were sculpted there. One of the chanting figures stepped forward and produced a human skull, which he held high over his head like some infernal crown. The chanting subsided, becoming a low, continuous moan in an instant. Mara did not think she had ever heard such an evil, primal, and base sound in all her life. It transpired that it was a fitting soundtrack to the unfolding horrors below, as the hooded man plunged the skull into the fountain and retrieved it. Mara stifled a gasp of terror. The skull was dripping crimson with blood.

Mara felt bile rush to her throat as she watched the cloaked figures each drink from the skull before passing it to their neighbour. That was enough for poor Mara, who staggered back and away from the hideous ritual of the death cult, their droning chants reaching new and darker ecstasies as she dashed back through the archway and ran as fast as she could away from them.

CHAPTER FOURTEEN

Lady Sophia emerged from the secret passageway via an alcove that was hidden behind a vast, musty wall hanging. Taking care to keep to the shadows, she took stock of her surroundings.

The corridor was well worn, suggesting it was, or had been, in near constant use. Good. A busy thoroughfare in a castle of this size meant she had found the more civilised area of the building. Lit torches running the length of the corridor seemed to testify to her assessment, in addition to the delicious waft of cooking smells emanating henceforth. She glanced around nervously, searching the shadows for intruders. Satisfied that she was alone, at least for now, she continued on toward the source of the delicious scents, her mouth watering at their possibilities. The atmosphere became warmer the further she walked, and this had a pleasing effect on her old bones. It was as though she were becoming invigorated by the smell and heat of a freshly cooked meal without even eating it.

The passageway widened into an antechamber that was lined with wooden chests, sacks, and wide shelves that drooped beneath the weight of earthenware vessels of all shapes and sizes. Seeing remnants of grain at the burst seam of one of the sacks, Lady Sophia felt a new pang of dread at the prospect of encountering a mouse – or worse still, a filthy rat – and quickly moved on through this enormous pantry. Another doorway between the shelves led her out into another passage, strewn with straw that rustled beneath her feet as she crossed it. A wide doorway from the passage led into a huge kitchen, and here the enticing scents of cooking overtook her completely. Lady Sophia drifted into the vast space as though floating upon a magic carpet of the senses.

The flames of an open hearth licked at a roasting boar and the crackling glistened in the orange flames, which hissed as salty fat dripped from the meat. A cauldron of steaming stew bubbled over another fire, forming the centrepiece of the room, and Lady Sophia watched steam curl upwards into giant copper pans that hung from hooks above. An ancient oak table stood along the far side of the kitchen, busy with cooking implements of all kinds, and festooned with bunches of fragrant dried herbs. A young maidservant stood at the other end of the table, seemingly oblivious to Lady Sophia's presence. As the aristocrat stepped closer, she saw that the girl was decanting a small wooden cask of wine into a crystal decanter. The light from the flames made the crystal twinkle like all the stars of a winter's night. The sound of the wine being poured was a veritable song. Lady Sophia licked her lips involuntarily.

The startled maid whirled around, sloshing wine across the table. "Oh! You gave me quite the fright, miss! Are you lost? I shall call for Master Klove to help you."

"Master Klove has given all the assistance he is willing to, I fear," Lady Sophia snapped, "and all that I am willing to accept, I hasten to add."

"Well, you're not supposed to be down here," the impetuous maid replied. "More than my job's worth—"

"Then, dear girl, I suggest you do your job and attend to your guest."

The maid looked dumbstruck. Or perhaps she just looked dumb. Her fingernails were chipped and revoltingly dirty, the bones poking through malnourished flesh. The girl's clothes were just as unkempt, and her teeth looked to be clinging on by some feat of gravity known only to those below stairs in this hellish backwater.

"Wine, girl," Lady Sophia ordered. "I am quite parched."

The maid's eyes widened, and then narrowed into dark slits of spite. "Why don't you help yourself, you old bag," the maid exclaimed, before turning on her heel and stomping away.

Lady Sophia gasped at the wretch's ill manners as the impetuous girl slammed the door behind her. She had only ever witnessed such bold rudeness from a maidservant once before in her life, and that had not ended well for the miscreant! Weak from her exertions, and exhausted by this vile castle and its inhabitants, she applied her mind to matters of immediate survival. Now that she had been left alone in the kitchen, she decided that she would do exactly as the maid had suggested. Retrieving a goblet, she filled it with wine from the decanter. The liquid was the same deep red colour as the velvet drapes Lady Sophia had so admired in the master suite. She lifted the goblet to her noble nose. The bouquet was complex. Deep, earthy tones, a hint of sweetness to it, but intoxicating in its full-bodied intensity. She put the cool crystal to her lips and took an investigative sip. The wine was so very well-rounded that it actually felt heavy in her mouth. Extraordinary. She let it wash over her tongue, her eyes closing as rivulets of heady flavour caressed her taste buds. Goodness gracious, if it wasn't the finest wine she had ever tasted.

She glanced idly around the kitchen, her wine-invigorated senses picking out hitherto unseen little details here and there. A clutch of beetroot, still encrusted with soil, hung from a hook above the preparation area. Their fat, purple forms looked like human hearts. Below them, on the table, a cleaver gleamed atop a thick wooden chopping board, stained red with the juices of beetroot or meat, she could not tell.

Strange; she had no recollection of refilling her glass, but it seemed full to the brim of its own accord. Lady Sophia felt a flush of warmth in her cheeks, and the acidity of hunger lapping at her insides. Her eyes wandered to the bubbling cauldron hanging over the fire, followed soon after by her feet.

The cauldron of steaming stew bubbled before her, flames dancing around its black, metallic base. The broth smelled delicious, rustic, and salty. Lady Sophia's stomach growled with a wine-induced hunger that was impossible to ignore. She crossed to the old oak table and found a silver spoon amidst the cutlery and other kitchen utensils stacked there. Wiping the spoon on her clothing – one could never be too careful – she returned to the cauldron. Filling the spoon with broth, she blew on its contents and the deliciously scented steam billowed around her already rosy cheeks. The taste was pure, slightly scalding, heaven. The broth was over seasoned, of course, perhaps to disguise a cheap cut of preserved meat, but it was the perfect complement to the richness of the wine. So much so that it warranted another spoonful.

But as she was about to follow her hunger's primal instruction and plunge the spoon back into the stew, Lady Sophia heard something that stopped her dead in her tracks. It was a plaintive sobbing, coming from some as yet unexplored corner of the kitchen. The sound made all the hairs stand up on the back of her neck. She dropped the spoon in fright and it fell into the stew-pot with a wet plop. Air bubbles rose to the surface of the broth, bringing with them what looked like an onion. But, as the orb righted itself atop the steaming lake of stew, she saw that it was not a vegetable at all, but an eyeball. A human eyeball, floating in the food she had just partaken of, its optic nerves wriggling in the bubbling broth like living tendrils!

Lady Sophia cried out as other ingredients floated quickly to the surface, revealing their drear and hideous natures. Strands of vein floated alongside severed fingers, the wounds where they had been chopped off grown soft and jellylike from simmering in the cauldron. Wisps of human hair swam around fragments of bone and – perhaps worst of all – a small collection of blackened teeth made tiny islands in the vile liquid. This was all too much for Lady Sophia's already distressed digestive system and, try as she might to fight it, she retched and vomited into the cauldron, spilling still-warm broth and spools of thick red wine into the abhorrent mixture.

Retreating in shocked surprise from the foulness of the cauldron, Lady Sophia collided with some pots and pans, and screamed in fresh alarm at their cacophonous report. Her movement startled an enormous rat, which thundered across the table, upsetting the cutlery and knocking it to the floor with deafening clashes and clatters. Lady Sophia staggered away from the cauldron, eager to be away from this unholy place and its furnace heat. Perspiration clouded her vision and she almost fell over her chair as she bolted for the kitchen door. Strange, it had been wide open when she had arrived. To her rising panic, she found it was locked. She pushed and pulled the handle and banged her fists against the door, but it was no use. The spiteful maidservant must have locked her in here, to what end, Lady Sophia did not wish to discover.

Retracing her steps, she continued past the table this time, toward the benches and shelves at the back of the kitchen.

The whimpering she had heard before came again, louder and incredibly close. She looked in the direction of the piteous sound and saw, with shock and horror, that it was coming from within a cage. The cage was shrouded in shadow, and so Lady Sophia took one of the flaming torches from its wall bracket. As she neared the rusty bars of the cage, movement startled her. Then, the torch flame revealed two wide and innocent eyes, blinking at her from behind the bars.

It was a child. A girl, no older than ten. Her tiny fingers gripped the metal bars in terror and anticipation. The poor child's face was so grimy that it was indistinguishable from the shadows. Here was an infant, so afraid that Lady Sophia's own fear began to subside as her protective instincts strode to the fore. Through heavy sobs, the girl began to plead with Lady Sophia in a language that she could not understand, but which spoke only of fear.

"English?" Lady Sophia asked. "Do you speak English, child?"

The girl blinked the tears from her desperate eyes. She stammered in a frantic gibberish of unrecognisable words, her voice laden with such childish innocence that it made Lady Sophia gasp. The girl was frantic, pulling against the bars of the cage and then pointing wildly between them in the direction of the door.

Finally, the child found the words. "Help!" she squealed, "Must hurry! They will come back!" And then, with a warning that almost stopped Lady Sophia's heart, she said, "They eat people here!"

CHAPTER FIFTEEN

*M*y blood burns and freezes all at once in my poisoned veins. Images rush through my mind in a whirlwind of colours. My heartbeat thunders in my ears, slowing all the while, until finally, it stops.

So this is death? It is quieter than I have imagined. All about me is void, and I am nothing within it. In life, I have become accustomed to keeping to the shadows. In the hereafter, must I do the same? I strive to find answers, but even my thoughts seem hollow in this nowhere space.

I close my eyes, or at least remember how that felt, and feel my consciousness retreating into the deeper recesses of memory. I hear a faint sound, drawing near. Or perhaps I am the one drawing nearer to it? It is the sound of horses' hooves against cobblestones, the self-same report that accompanied my formative years in London. No sooner have I thought of the place I once called home than it begins to take definable shape in my mind. I can hear the cry of the fishmonger and the hubbub of the crowd as it bustles around Spitalfields Market. I hear the tinkling of piano keys from The Princess Alice pub. The dirty laughter of the street women. I remember the stupid names they gave themselves. Long Susan. Tall Sally. Lucky Nell.

I yearn to punish them, and then erase them all.

The crying of a baby focuses my memories on a window on the ground floor of a town house. I see through the window, into the room behind it. A babe in arms lies cradled by his mother. She whispers to him and strokes his skin, telling him that everything will be all right.

She lies.

She always lies.

It will not be all right. And I know that she is the cause of this. Her pathetic addiction to gin, that and the base profession she has lowered herself to in order to fund it, have ruined any chance we had of ascending from the slum I was born into. Oh, and here they come again, her whispered sweet nothings about how my father is a higher-up of noble blood, no less, and how he will take care of us!

We'll want for nothing.

He's a prince among men.

She's in thrall of him.

But all he's given her is a death sentence. And me. One and the same, you might say. Soon, my soft cheek turns scabrous with the taint of syphilis. Only rotten fruit could grow in her diseased womb. She's so bleedin' pickled she doesn't even notice. I grow, and become one with my affliction. It doesn't kill me like it does her. The bats in her belfry have well and truly come home to roost by the time they cart her off to the knacker's yard, and me to the workhouse.

We learn to co-exist, my scars and I.

Months pass, until someone comes for me. I am put to work. I am fed. When I am not working, or eating, I sleep. And

I dream. The dream is always the same. It is of a higher purpose. The sickness that courses through my veins was meant to kill me. My bedclothes are stained yellow with it each morning. And yet, I still live.

When I become a man, I realise why. The awareness has been germinating within me for quite some time, before blossoming like a flower. Higher purpose. I will rid the world of other gin-soaked, syphilitic sops like my dear old ma. Yes, I know all the stupid names they have given themselves. Stage names for actors who only know the one role. I begin to observe their world from within, charting a map of their ruin. As a child, I'm the glass collector. They don't even see me. As a young man, I work as a gopher for the man up the road. They don't see me then, either. When I'm good and ready for them to see me, I'm installed as a surgeon's apprentice. He says I'm the best he's ever had because I stand by, all quiet like, and never faint or puke when he opens one up. He teaches me everything I need to know about their cankerous insides and how best to put a stop to them.

I've got my bag of tricks, now, and have accumulated all the knowledge I require to put them to good use doing God's work. For God has abandoned the East End. My blade becomes the lesson. The flock is ill-prepared to receive it. But receive it, they shall.

Berner Street is a close call. They almost have eyes on me at that one, the Old Bill. But still, they don't see me. Someone sends letters, and a liver, even, and that sends them into a right old froth. All for the greater good because it leaves me to get my head down for a bit while they chase their own tail.

The last one is the best. I really make her listen.

"It'll be all right, dear," she says, to me, or to herself, I don't know. And I don't care. "It'll be all right." Just like me dear old ma used to say. Well, those are her last words as it

goes. She's still breathing when I take her guts out in front of her and then hold them up so she can see.

"It will not be all right," I say.

"It will never be all right, until every last stinking one of you is gone from this earth."

And I'm the man for the job.

Old Jacky.

I'm in the room with her again. I can smell her. Sweet release. I glance over at the bedside table where I have deposited her severed parts. No use to her anymore. I look down at my apron, slick with her blood. I can feel my knife, sturdy and true in my ripping hand. The floorboards look black beside the bed where she's bled out. Her face hangs open and it's as though her skull is simply wearing a mask.

Well, don't we all?

I go to wipe the knife on the bedclothes but hesitate.

I never hesitate, so why now?

I raise the knife to my mouth and, before I even know what I'm doing, I lick the blood from the blade. It tastes delicious. Sweet, salty nectar that makes my tastebuds do a dance on the back of my tongue! This is new. I have never—

And then I feel only horror and revulsion at what I have done. I have taken her poisoned blood into my body. It's a violation of all that is holy. It is a mockery of my higher purpose! I bend double and heave her blood up onto the floorboards. Hot tears flood my vision and I wail in anguish at the idea that even a single droplet of her blood remains within my person. I cough. I rage. I splutter. I writhe in agony on the floor, deep in the agonizing and uncontrollable throes of one of my seizures. I open my eyes.

I am no longer in Kelly's lodging house. The floorboards are now stone slabs. I roll over onto my back and see a vaulted ceiling above me. To one side, I can see a high window. It is barred against the starlit sky. To the other I can see a stone dais and around it, set onto plinths, a number of coffins.

> *Is this Hell?*
>
> *Did I not do enough good work to please You?*

I crawl to my feet. I feel lighter, somehow. A glance down at my hands, alabaster white. Blood-tainted vomit stains the floor at my feet, a mark of shame. I walk over to the coffins and find one of them open, a thin layer of soil within. Beside it, there are three other coffins.

It is only then that I remember the trio of quiet women who violated me in the boudoir. Fragments of memory return to me, like shards of the broken mirror. I recall the unwelcome kiss of their fangs and it freezes me at my neck and wrist once more. Seeking my wounds out with my fingertips, I find none. The flesh has healed over, renewed, and it feels softer than ever. Even softer than when I was a babe, before Ma's sickness fruited within me from the poison seed of her unholy union with my father. And all the rest of them. I know then that I am changing beneath the skin, as well as upon its surface. The sickness that I have known symbiosis with all my life is leaving me. I can feel it diminishing even now, an old friend and combatant growing ever distant. I do not want it to go. Yet go, it does.

A new sickness worms its way inside of me. A hunger more profound than I knew even when I was in the gutter, hunting for scraps. It churns in my stomach and burns in my throat. And yet, even in the deathlike spasms of that all-consuming hunger I can feel a new power within me. A dark force surging through my veins and taking hold as a master puppeteer might command the strings of his marionette. A voice, darker still, whispers somewhere deep within my psyche. It tells me that everything will be all right. And this time, I believe it. If only I can satiate this bloody hunger. I am famished. I must feed.

"All in good time," the voice tells me. "First, you must sleep. Let the power grow within you. Sleep, and then arise renewed."

Instinct draws me to the open coffin, and the bed of soil within. I run my fingers through it. Strange, my nails seem longer, and sharper than once they were. I climb into the coffin and pull the lid shut over me. As darkness envelops me in its velvet embrace, I succumb to it.

I am a stranger, and mine is a stranger's tale.

For I am a stranger now even to myself.

CHAPTER SIXTEEN

The ringing in Grayson's ears pealed louder than a tolling bell.

His cheek felt numb and, opening first one eye and then the other, he saw that he was lying face down on a cold stone floor. He grimaced as he rolled over onto his back, feeling a stab of pain at the rear of his skull where he had been struck. The ceiling above him was made of solid grey stone also. This was not the courtyard where he had fallen. The black-clad occultists must have brought him here. But where, by gad, was here? The air was damp and musty, and the temperature at a level perhaps better suited to denizens of the Arctic.

Grayson guessed that he was "below stairs" so to speak.

Oh, how the mighty had fallen.

He sat up, feeling queasy to the pit of his stomach as he did so. They had bashed him quite severely on the noggin. He hadn't experienced a head quite as sore as this one since he'd had that run-in with a publican over the poor fellow's daughter. Grayson had made an emergency exit of the buxom young lass's window, but had misjudged the distance between boudoir above and hay cart below. That, coupled with a monstrous three-day hangover, had put him in the infirmary for the best part of a week. Still, there was always a bright side, that time provided by a delectable nurse with hands soft as silk and a more than generous bedside manner.

Would that he were in a nice warm bed under the care of a trained medical professional now, instead of abandoned, beaten and bruised upon a hard stone floor!

Glancing around, Grayson's eyes began to take in the full extent of his predicament. A pittance of straw, strewn across the floor, was the only thing even approaching comfort in this cold, hard little cell. For a cell it most certainly was. Worst of all, in the corner to his right lay a skeleton, still manacled to chains that hung heavy from the wall. The yellow bones at the wrists had turned an oxidised blue-green against their irons.

Panicking, Grayson sought out any sign of an exit from this damnable hellscape. His eyes were growing accustomed to the low light levels, but all he could see were floor-to-ceiling bars opposite where he sat.

He shuffled over to them, groaning all the while in protest at his injuries. He gripped the bars and pulled at them. He felt the rising panic of the incarcerated innocent. He, an officer and a gentleman, thrown into a death trap of a dungeon like a common miscreant! It was an outrage. Those hooded chaps had no business treating an Englishman of his breeding stock in such a manner.

Grayson's fevered brain cycled back to the strange, arcane happenings he had witnessed in the courtyard. He had posed no threat to them, no, none at all! All he had bally well been trying to do was leave the premises before their damnable ceremony, or whatever it was, reached its crescendo. He had chosen the most polite and respectable option available to him – a quiet withdrawal – and look how they had repaid him for it. The bounders! One thing he'd learned during his years abroad was that religious extremists, and the extremely religious, had little in the way of patience with those they earmarked as unbelievers.

And it was disbelief that gripped him now as he heard the creak of a door, followed by heavy footfalls on some faraway stair. Someone was coming. Perhaps most disturbing of all was the grinding sound of metal against stone that accompanied each step.

Step-scrape. Step-scrape. Step-scrape.

As the evil sounds grew nearer, Grayson saw the undulating glow of torchlight illuminate the passage outside his cell. With it came an enormous shadow that made Grayson gasp for breath and back away from the bars. For the shadow was of a giant of a man and, dragging on the floor behind him, the unmistakable silhouette of an axe. So, that was the source of the infernal scraping sound. Had they sent his executioner? He had missed the part where he had a fair trial, somehow.

Grayson's acute sense of self-preservation propelled him back into the cell until he was standing with his back against the wall near the spot where he had first regained consciousness. He wondered if there was enough straw to hide beneath. Or, and he trembled at the thought, enough at least to staunch a wound. The sinking pit of his stomach told him that the skeleton in the cell would have a bedfellow before long.

When he saw the size of the axe, terror gripped him. Such a weapon was designed for one thing, and one thing only: to lop off the limbs of whatever its bearer wished to fell. And, Grayson suspected, not just those belonging to trees. Oh no. No ordinary man could even lift such a weapon! As the executioner held the torch aloft to peer in at his prey, who stood trembling in his cell, Grayson saw the man's face.

It was the American. The chap with the enormous hands and the Teutonic name which, understandably, had slipped his mind for the present.

"Praise be to Heaven," Grayson said, as surprised as the next man to have apparently found God at this juncture. "You've come to save me from this infernal place. And not a moment too soon, dear fellow!"

The American eyed Grayson dispassionately. For a few awkward moments he just stood there, staring at him, and Grayson wondered if the man might up and leave him to his fate. Then, the American leaned the enormous axe up against the wall. He inserted the flaming torch into a vacant wall bracket and then turned his attention to the cell bars.

"No use old fellow. I'm locked in," Grayson said. "I say, perhaps you can use that splendid axe of yours to bend the bars?"

The American stared at him, and it was as though he saw through Grayson – right through to the other side. The man's eyes twinkled blue, and with some form of preternatural power. This fellow saw into darker places than Grayson cared to venture. Feeling uneasy in the path of that glare, he began to wonder what the American planned to do with his oversized, limb-severing axe. Perhaps Grayson was safer locked in the cell after all?

Then, the giant man reached out and gripped the bars with both hands before pulling them toward him, hard. To Grayson's surprise, and with a squeak of rust, they moved! The American pulled again, grunting with effort as he did so, and the bars swung open.

There had been an unlocked gate right in front of him all along.

"If only I'd thought of that," Grayson muttered, making a mental note to do exactly that if he ever found himself behind bars again. An outcome he sincerely wished to avoid in future – if at all possible.

"I really cannot thank you enough, old chap," Grayson blustered.

The American stepped inside the cell and stomped toward him. Crikey, he seemed even larger in the confines of the cell, if such a thing were possible.

"I could have starved down here for all they care," Grayson continued, "Come, let's—"

The giant hand at his throat cut off his next words before they had formed in his mouth. Grayson gasped for breath and found none. Dragged forward, he kicked his feet wildly in a futile attempt to gain traction on the stone floor. The American's fingers closed tighter around Grayson's cravat. Dangling, helpless, he was pulled unceremoniously from his cell by the giant and out into the passageway. Pausing only to grab a hold of his terrifying axe, the American strode on, dragging Grayson along with him. This was a far cry from the jailbreak that Grayson had envisaged when his surly rescuer had come a-calling.

"I say, there's absolutely no need to be so rough about it," Grayson protested in between gasping for his next breath, "I'm grateful to you of course ... For saving me ... Believe me I am ... Trust me, I'll come quietly ... There's no need ..."

His protests fell on deaf ears. The American remained silent and stoic as a statue beneath the brim of his enormous hat. They reached a corner and Grayson lost his footing as the brute dragged him round it like a ragdoll. It was of no consequence. The American's physique was that of a circus strongman. He could drag Grayson any which way without even flinching. Grayson did flinch, however, when he saw the nightmarish destination to which his dubious rescuer had hauled him.

CHAPTER SEVENTEEN

L ady Sophia's mind raced. How could she free this poor captive child?

"Be brave, child. Wait. I shall locate the key to your prison."

With that, Lady Sophia took her flaming torch and began searching every nook and cranny in the kitchen, but to no avail. She was considering trying to prise the bars open with the poker from the fire when she heard the child whimper in terror. The girl's rising fear was entirely justified, for Lady Sophia heard footfalls approaching. Her glance in the direction of the door was entirely fortuitous for, hidden in plain sight until now, she saw a metal hoop with keys attached hanging from the adjacent wall. Lady Sophia retrieved it as quickly as her old bones would allow, and rushed back to the cage where the young girl was in an apoplexy of terror. Lady Sophia judged the smallest key to be the likeliest suspect, and allowed herself a small moment of victory when it did indeed turn inside the lock. The grubby child pushed against the bars and the cage door swung open, almost knocking Lady Sophia from her feet. But it was too late. She heard another key rattle in the lock of the door to the kitchen behind them.

"I know a secret way, hurry!" urged the girl, before grabbing hold of Lady Sophia's hand and leading her toward the back of the kitchen.

When they reached a line of storage cabinets along the wall, the girl let go of her hand, stooped and opened one. The back of the cupboard had rotted away, revealing a narrow crawlspace beyond. Lady Sophia steeled herself before stooping and following the girl through the opening, almost at a crawl and with the flaming torch held out in front of her. Once they were both safely through, the child crawled back, reached through the opening and pulled the cupboard door shut. They had made it.

Relieved to be free of the claustrophobia-inducing crawl, Lady Sophia stood erect, wincing at the sounds of her vertebrae clicking in protest. She held up the torch and saw that this "secret way" had led them into a narrow pantry, its shelves bare save for dozens of cobwebs that hung heavy with dust. Breathless from their frantic escape, they both stood in the pantry for a few moments before proceeding through an opening and out into a dank corridor. The castle walls were slimy with moisture down here, and there was an unpleasantly damp smell, which carried with it an even more unpleasant charnel odour. Lady Sophia took a handkerchief from her cuff and held it over her nose to quell the stench. It was as though they had flown from Hell's kitchen only to find themselves within its drain.

"Do you know a way out of here, child?"

The girl looked for all the world as though it were Lady Sophia speaking a foreign language and, she reflected, she supposed she was. She put her handkerchief away and held her fingers up to the torchlight. She mimed walking with her fingers, creating a shadow play on the wall. The girl watched, transfixed, and the Lady Sophia mimed taking a deep breath of fresh air.

"Out?" she said to the girl, "Out of the castle?"

The girl's eyes took on a decidedly more determined aspect and she nodded before saying, "Yes. I know the secret ways. You follow me."

The child led her on, through ever-narrowing corridors and twisting spiral steps, down into the very bowels of the castle. The air dripped with damp, and cold began to clutch at Lady Sophia's bones. Finally, the girl slowed her pace. She came to a halt at the end of the passageway and pointed at a dark hole in the wall. It looked like the masonry had come down some years ago. A breach in the wall that must lead …

"Out," the girl said.

"You clever, clever girl," Lady Sophia replied. "Come along, then."

As she neared the hole, Lady Sophia paused for a moment on instinct, and glanced back at the girl.

"Come along, I said," repeated Lady Sophia, but the child did not budge.

The girl glanced nervously back from whence they had come. "They are coming!" she whispered frantically.

Lady Sophia turned from the opening, holding her torch aloft and squinting to see over the child's head, into the distance.

"I don't see anyone, child, are you sure—"

She looked down at her young charge and saw the child's mouth curl into a vicious grin. Her teeth were almost blood red in the flickering torch flame. A flash of murder glimmered darkly in the girl's eyes, which now looked older, beyond her years.

Then the child shoved her, hard, and Lady Sophia fell back through the hole in the wall.

And she did not stop falling.

CHAPTER EIGHTEEN

Grayson's panicked eyes seemed encircled by threats too numerous to count, his body wracked with pain from the bludgeoning, from his fall, and now from being dragged by a giant toward his very doom.

The dank, dungeon chamber into which the American had delivered him was a macabre museum of man's worst nightmares come true. Blood trickled between the cracks of the stone floor, pooling into drain covers stained dark crimson. Grayson swallowed at the sight of so much lifeblood spilling away like red rainfall into the storm drains of Hell itself.

The atmosphere within the chamber was that of carnivalesque putrefaction. Hot, sweet air drifted through unseen cracks in the walls, and with it came a heady, salty scent, like fat dripping from a suckling pig and roasting on hot coals. This pungent olfactory blend reminded Grayson of a village fair he had attended long ago, where a spit roast had crackled beside a candyfloss vendor's confections. Here, in this chamber, the scents only gave rise to primal threats within him as he tried not to imagine their source.

His heels slipped and skidded in wet blood as the American dragged him further inside, and he cried out at the unbearable throb of pain inside his skull, but to no avail. Passing a statuesque form that stood near the wall, Grayson thought at first that he was looking at a sarcophagus of some kind. But he let out a whimper when he saw vicious spikes through the slightly opened door. It was an iron maiden! What base savagery must this dismal place have witnessed, Grayson wondered, before feeling terror strike him hard as a deathblow to think that he might be its next victim.

His right foot snagged on something and he looked down to see a length of coiled rope. It too was stained rosy red with blood, and looked disturbingly like a noose that had frayed away and detached from the weight of too many victims. Dangling helplessly from the man's massive fist, Grayson watched as the American placed his giant axe in the pool of blood where the rope lay discarded. He felt a chill at the fact that the huge man was apparently oblivious to such horrors. In fact, the goliath seemed utterly at ease with his nightmarish surroundings, strolling on past the lurid tableaux of implements and sordid spillages, and all the while hauling Grayson along with him.

Reaching a lone chair at the centre of the chamber, the American lifted him into it. Grayson's arms and legs tried to protest, to wriggle free independently of their owner, but it was of no use. The sturdy wooden chair had been furnished with thick leather straps at wrist and ankle, and the American set about fastening them. He did it without a care for comfort, the leather straps biting into Grayson's flesh with all the ferocity of jungle snakes.

"I say, old chap, that's a little forward. We've only just met," Grayson quipped. Yet he was unable to disguise the rising panic in his voice.

In reply, the American simply grunted as he fastened the remaining straps. And then, when Grayson was tightly bound to the chair, he took a couple of steps back as though surveying his grim handiwork.

To the right of the American stood a table bearing a disturbing array of instruments. Grayson's heart beat a little faster with each detail his unwitting eye alighted upon. A rusty syringe, its glass tube containing a vividly green liquid, the purpose of which Grayson could not even guess. A coil of metal chain links sat in a slick of congealing blood and, beside it, a barbed whip, each thorny tip dripping yet more lifeblood onto the scarred metal surface of the table. Grayson averted his eyes from these horrors and in doing so, found yet more of them. A ball and chain lay beside one of the table legs, with – sweet Jesus! – a severed foot still attached, the skin a hideous yellowy grey colour. The wound above the ankle was a livid red. It looked as though the foot had been torn off, such was the extent of the trauma to the surrounding flesh. Its former owner must have bled to death – or worse. If there were such a thing.

The air in the chamber was thick with the metallic scent of blood, that disturbing salt-sweetness, and with the unmistakeable musk of fear. His fear. They were all too familiar scents to Grayson, who had spent much of his adult life being afraid and so had run away from several blood-drenched battlefields in his time. To meet his maker here, amidst the very apparatus of suffering and death, was anathema to him. He'd always rather fancied that he would shuffle off his particular mortal coil comfortably warm in bed, looking back on his various conquests with no regrets save for the lack of one last, almighty hurrah.

But here? In this pit of despair? He could almost feel a lifetime of unwanted regrets queueing up outside the door to inflict their misery upon him.

"What Hell is this, sir!?" Grayson really could not bear it any longer. The door was all too visible to him from his enforced seated position. He wished he could somehow transport himself through it and away from this awful place. Again, he saw the severed foot in its anklet of iron and shuddered.

"I see you are disturbed by the ball and chain."

The voice was insidiously calm, almost musical in quality, and coming from somewhere behind Grayson. He tried to turn his head in order to see the speaker, but the high back of the chair against his head injury, coupled with the restraint of his fastenings, only afforded him a repeat viewing of the terrifying iron maiden.

"Worry not, I can assure you we cauterised the wound," the unseen narrator continued.

The most disturbing thing about a voice like that, Grayson thought, *is its calmness in a place such as this. It means that the speaker is entirely at ease here. Imagine being at home amidst such torture, pain, and filth!*

Sudden, brisk movement at his ear made Grayson flinch, and he heard the swish of robes as the speaker passed close by him – too close.

"He died of natural causes an hour or two later," the man concluded.

Grayson's heart sank further upon seeing the speaker's frightening visage. He looked to be well into his fifth decade, perhaps even his sixth, but his eyes looked youthfully sharp in the torchlight. A fierce intelligence burned bright behind them along with something else – cruelty. That cruel aspect seemed to emanate from him in dark waves that chilled Grayson to his marrow.

He was clad from neck to floor in vivid, red robes, and the obsidian prayer beads that hung about his neck struck new and more fervent terror into Grayson's already palpitating heart. If this fellow was religious as well as cruel then it would surely spell disaster for a poor heathen such as he.

But it was the American to whom this red-robed inquisitor turned his attention next, for the beastly man held out his hand in some silent, cryptic prompt.

The inquisitor smiled, his lips stretching until they formed a razor-thin slash across his pale features. Reaching inside the folds of his robes, he produced an object that glittered in the light from the wall torches. It was a small bottle of clear liquid, the ornate silver cap engraved with a cruciform.

"This will serve you well, my child," the red-robed man oiled in that sickly sweet voice.

The American held the bottle up to the light, inspecting it, and then, apparently satisfied with regard to its provenance, secreted it within the pockets of his greatcoat. Then, to Grayson's dismay, the huge man turned on his heel and retrieved his enormous axe before striding purposefully out of the chamber.

"No! Wait! Don't leave me here! I beg of you!"

Grayson's protestations were futile. The American lumbered from view without so much as a backward glance. *The bounder! Leaving me strapped to a chair in a torture chamber, alone with some sadistic lunatic.* It was more than Grayson's poor, reeling mind could bear. He struggled against his straps again, but it was no use. They gripped him tight as a vice.

"Don't struggle," the man said, "plenty of time for that later."

"Who are you, sir? With what authority do you imprison me here? I am a gentleman of Her Majesty, and an honoured guest here in this castle. I demand that you loosen these straps immediately."

Grayson's bravado seemed to take the strange man off guard. His sharp little eyes widened in surprise at Grayson's outburst. Grayson thought for a brief, beautiful moment that the man might yet do his bidding, but then he simply threw back his head and laughed. The laugh, rather like the man's speaking voice, was laconic. It was as though Grayson had made some quip or other over billiards after luncheon.

"Well, I must confess, I fail to see what might be so funny, sir."

"Confess," chuckled the red-robed man. "Yes, you will confess when I am done with you."

At that, Grayson fell quiet. The frog of fear had taken residency in his throat once more.

"You claim you are a gentleman, an honoured guest," the man went on, "yet I put it to you that you are neither. You are a deserter, a coward, and a cheat. The only reason you are still alive and sitting in that chair is because I will it. You ask what authority I have here? Well, my dear gentleman, I am the very definition of the word. I am your inquisitor. You will do well to respond to my questions quickly, and with the utmost honesty. The time for playing the part of the bumbling charmer is over. Here, in my chamber, you are base matter. You are the meat, and I am the tenderiser."

These last words shocked a whimper from Grayson's throat. How could this bounder know quite so much about him? He sat watching, helpless in the chair, as the inquisitor strolled over to the metal table and began idly searching through the implements there with the tips of his black-leather-gloved fingers. Whatever he was looking for, Grayson hoped against hope that the fellow had misplaced it somewhere.

No such luck.

"Ah-ha!" the inquisitor exclaimed.

The robed man turned his attention back to Grayson and held aloft an object so that Grayson could see it more clearly. It was fashioned from wood and metal, with two blocks conjoined by tarnished screws. At its centre, a butterfly screw had been partly tightened. It looked like a miniature flower press, but Grayson knew its true purpose in an instant. He had seen a ghastly contraption such as this during his time behind the lines when his superior officers had found it necessary to make some chap or other talk – once they had stopped screaming.

They were thumbscrews.

The inquisitor nodded and smiled that thin smile once more upon noticing Grayson's recognition of the dread device.

"Don't worry. Pain is all in the mind. These ruffians won't break you. Much."

And with that, the inquisitor placed the thumbscrews in Grayson's lap. A demonstration of power, and a most unwelcome intrusion. Grayson began to shiver uncontrollably. Seemingly oblivious, the red robed man began to unfasten one of the wrist straps. Grayson's fevered brain began processing wild ideas about fighting back, but what could he do? His ankles were still strapped to the bloody chair. In any case, the inquisitor inserted Grayson's thumb into the contraption before beginning to unfasten the other wrist strap.

It was almost as though he had done this before.

Second thumb secured between the crushing plates of the machine, the inquisitor stood to his full height again and looked down at Grayson with a sneer.

"Pain is all in the mind. And what a mind you have. Tsk, tsk! All those dirty little secrets! Imagine what might spill out when I—"

He lunged forward, fast as a dart, and set about turning the butterfly screw. Grayson felt his flesh being compressed in an instant. He ground his teeth as the crushing sensation bit into the bone beneath it.

"Please! I'll tell you anything! Anything you want to hear!"

Grayson flinched as much at his own weakness as the pain searing into his extremities.

"Goodness me but they don't often give up so quickly. What makes you think you have anything worth hearing?"

Grayson stammered, trying to find the words that might give this monster cause to stop. Then, he screamed as the inquisitor tightened the thumbscrews another full turn. His thumbs were burning, the heat of assault igniting his nerve endings and making molten lava of his forearms.

"I ... I ... I ..."

"Yammering fool! Spit it out, man. I am a busy man. Haven't got all night. I have other clients to tend to ..."

He tightened the screw once more. Grayson began to whimper. He didn't even care that hot tears were now flooding from his eyes. The pain was simply too great to endure. He shut his eyes tight and waited for the next attack.

Instead, he felt pressure at his left ankle. Opening one eye, he looked down to see the inquisitor crouching before him. The savage was unfastening his ankle strap. Had he relented? The relief of such a prospect almost stopped Grayson feeling the agony of the thumbscrews. Almost.

"Forgive me, I acted too hastily. Far too hastily. I'm not used to clients offering to spill their guts so soon. Not until after a little foreplay, anyhow. Especially British chaps like yourself. Stiff upper lip and all that. Yes, I've broken a few of those in my time. Admirable in their way, how heroic they seem at first. Until I locate their weak spot. But you ..." The inquisitor looked up at Grayson with the same look of disdain as a disappointed schoolmaster before continuing. "You are all weak spot, aren't you?"

Grayson did not deny it. But even in the midst of his humiliation some fight was returning to him. He so wanted to kick this sadist in the chops when his right foot was free. Wanted, despite his bowel-trembling fear of this man, to give him a sound thrashing. But the bounder knew what was up, and kept one hand on the thumbscrews while he finished unfastening the last strap. The inquisitor smiled, this time showing his teeth. They were yellow, and it seemed to Grayson that when he grinned so, this evil man was revealing a glimpse of the rot that festered at his foul core.

Grayson gasped as the man stood up and then pulled the thumbscrews upwards with him, forcing Grayson to stand. The pain was intense. It felt as though Grayson's thumbs might be twisted and snapped off at any moment. Unbearably, the red-robed man began to lead Grayson from the chair. His foot struck against something on the floor and he realised with sickening clarity that it was the traumatised foot attached to the ball and chain.

"Come along now," his cruel captor said, "I have just the thing for weak spots."

Gagging at the intensity of his own trauma, Grayson was led by his inquisitor across the stone floor of the chamber. The thumbscrews caused him to walk in the manner of a spasmodic puppet. Each step was more torturous than the last. Grayson wanted to ask where he was being taken, but no words would come, only animal sounds of pain that he barely recognised as human, let alone as emanating from his own person.

"Here we are," the inquisitor said, with all the joviality of a stationmaster announcing the last stop on a day trip to the seafront.

Grayson's eyes widened in panic. He felt his legs buckle beneath him as they had in the courtyard when he had been struck. In many ways, he wished someone could knock him out once more, to spare him the mortal terror of what stood before him.

The iron maiden.

The inquisitor pulled the door open to its full extent with his free hand, revealing row upon row of deadly, jutting spikes within.

Before Grayson could protest, the inquisitor shoved Grayson forward. Preservation instinct caused Grayson to turn and only then did the inquisitor let go of the thumbscrews. The man's strong hand grabbed onto Grayson's face, forcing him back against the spikes. Gasping, Grayson tried to pull his hands up in front of his body to defend himself, a wounded pigeon hiding behind its fragile wings. But the inquisitor already had a metal shackle around his wrist before he could react again. His captor snapped the metal shut, and then fastened another to Grayson's other wrist. Weak, sobbing in pain, Grayson tried not to slump inside the cabinet, feeling the hard points of the spikes at his back.

The inquisitor began closing the door on him.

"Please ..." Grayson tried to say, phlegm caught in his throat.

The door creaked mockingly as it continued to close. Grayson could see the inquisitor's face through the little window framed in iron in the door. Those thin lips were blurring into an angry red gash in Grayson's tear-filled vision. His eyes were vague wells of inky darkness. Impervious to his plight, indifferent to his pain.

"Please ... I'll do anything you ask ..." he begged. "Anything ..."

The red blur of the inquisitor's mouth widened, exposing those yellowing teeth once more. "Anything?" he said, as though it were some new and exotic foreign word he had never pronounced before.

"Anything," Grayson gasped. He could feel the jab of the door spikes against his torso now. Within seconds they would begin to pierce his flesh.

The door stopped closing.

Still, Grayson hardly dared breathe.

"Anything. Hmmm ..." the inquisitor mused. Agonising seconds passed, during which the red-robed man made a show of considering his options. Then he looked Grayson straight in the eye and said, "Atone."

"W ... what?" Grayson asked, dumbfounded.

"You must atone, man."

"B ... but h ... how?"

"Oh, by killing one of the others. You have lived your dubious life as a coward, have you not? Always leaving the fighting for someone else. Well, this is your chance to show your quality. To unburden yourself of your trivial little sins by committing the one act that you have, thus far, allowed others to do for you. You must atone. You must take the life of one of the other sinners."

"Which ... other?" The words sounded alien on Grayson's tongue, but they were his ticket to freedom from this vile torture chamber and its cruel master.

"You will do it, then? Good." The inquisitor opened the door fully and unfasted the manacles at Grayson's wrists. The thumbscrews still held his hands together in front of him.

The inquisitor took a few steps back, and then beckoned to Grayson to step out. But Grayson was too afraid to move.

"Come, choose your weapon."

Grayson willed his limbs to move and eventually they did. The pain at his thumbs had become a dull numbness. He tried to focus on the room beyond the threshold of the iron maiden instead. He took a few furtive steps after the inquisitor, who led him toward a corner table.

"What will it be?" his captor asked, and Grayson saw that the table was laden with the apparatus of murder in all its manifold forms. A mace lay alongside a rusty spear, beneath which lay a coil of garrotting wire. But it was the glint of steel that caught Grayson's eye. He pointed at the weapons as best he could with the thumbscrews attached.

"Oh, a fine choice! Two for the price of none!"

The inquisitor cackled in amusement, a horrid, high-pitched sound that sounded like a sack of cats being lowered into a firepit. Now that Grayson was almost free, he wanted to be as far away as possible from this odious and manipulative man.

"I had better remove those thumbscrews so that you may claim your prize," the inquisitor said in mock kindness.

Grayson bit his lip as his captor took the contraption into his hands once again. But in a sudden, the vile man had twisted the butterfly screw tighter! Grayson yelped in agony but was unable to move with his tender flesh trapped inside the infernal machine.

"If you fail to do as I have instructed, you will experience tortures the likes of which have never been visited upon a human being before; do you understand? I will give you your weapons, but first you will give me your word as an Englishman."

Grayson yelped in pain again as the inquisitor tightened the thumbscrews once more.

"Swear it, man! You will take the life of one of the other sinners in the castle!"

"I swear! I swear! On the King, the Queen, and all of their Royal offspring from this generation unto the next!" Grayson exclaimed, half-shouting and half-screaming.

The inquisitor released the thumbscrews and tore them away from Grayson's ruined thumbs. The sensation flooded back to his digits along with the flow of blood in his veins. By gad, it was the worst pain he had ever experienced. But he was still breathing. Without skipping a beat, the inquisitor discarded the thumbscrews and handed Grayson his weapons. First one, then the other. Grayson felt the cold weight of the butcher's knives in his hands.

Two for the price of none.

He looked down at the knives, and then at the livid cuts and bruises marking his damaged flesh and began to wonder who the easiest target might be. One of the women, obviously. The sharp-tongued Lady Sophia, perhaps. Or the delectable Mara. He felt a pang of regret at the thought of harming such a beauty. Lady Sophia, then. Yes. He'd much prefer to do away with the old lady. She was almost into the final pages of her memoirs anyway. Yes, he could lure her into a trap. She would trust a well-spoken English gent like him. *Bumbling*, the inquisitor had called him. Well, that affable act might come to the fore if he were to hit his mark this time!

He shuddered at the implication of such a thought.

"I say, where might I find the bedroom suites?"

Wincing at the pain in his hands as he tucked the butcher's knives into his belt, he looked around for an answer from the inquisitor – and found himself to be standing alone in the torture chamber.

It was as though some maniacal, vengeful spirit had visited him, only to disappear like a mere figment of the imagination.

CHAPTER NINETEEN

I awake in darkness that is both outside and inside of me. Hunger gnaws at my stomach like an ulcer, and I try to curl in a ball to contain the anguish. My knees hit a solid surface and I remember where I am. I can smell the soil beneath me, a richly pungent distillation of life and death. Reaching up with one hand, I find the lid of the coffin and push.

The other coffins are still closed and I know now that the three unholy women who attacked me slumber within them. My old instincts return, a rush of mortal desire to cut, to slice, to re-educate. I clamber out of the coffin and search the shadows for something sharp with which to do my work. Never has my vision been so clear in such relative darkness. I have always been a creature of the shadows, but not like this. I can see every hidden detail. A spider moves across its web in the corner of the vaulted ceiling. A bat flits across the sky beyond the high, barred window. These night creatures are my kith and kin. And the three women? I cannot bear the thought of their tainted blood running through my veins. But, as I move toward their coffins I can feel that blood speaking to my very being, holding me back from doing them harm. The dark gift they have bestowed upon me has made them my kith and kin, also. They are sisters to the night, and I, their unwitting brother. My knife hand twitches – the muscle memory of an anticipated kill. My blood is up.

Our blood.

I force my fingers to curl, instead, into a fist. I feel how sharp my teeth have become against my lips. Curious. I run my tongue across the points of my incisors, and begin to yearn for another kind of reckoning.

Turning my back on the coffins, I move to the stairs. I feel weightless. Walking is no effort at all. I am at the top of the stairs before I have even decided to climb them, it seems. I am dazzled by my own speed, and then by my lithe movements into the corridor beyond the doorway that leads back to the vault.

Hearing a sound like crashing thunder, I pause for a moment in the passageway. A rat scurries by, screeching as it goes. Its claws against the stone sound as loud as thunderclaps to my ears. The power that courses through my veins seems to have given me more than speed and dexterity. I can hear as sharply as I can see. The whole castle seems to explode into life upon each of my senses. I can sense the heat of bodies larger than the rat's moving somewhere ahead of me. My legs take me in their direction, driven by some primal instinct. As I emerge onto the balustrade above an open courtyard, I can hear heartbeats loud as the drums of a marching band. I stop and listen intently, deciphering each overlapping beat. There are four of them. Men. I hear their low murmurs to each other as they attend to their menial tasks in the courtyard. One is breaking barrels, another chopping the wood with a hand axe.

The third tosses the cut wood onto a fire, beside which the fourth warms his hands. He must be their master.

I smell their sweat.

Yet strongest of all, I smell their blood.

I grip the crenelated wall of the ledge and peer over from the shadows. They are far below, stacking boxes and barrels at the corner of the courtyard, oblivious to my presence. Before I even know I am doing it, I am crawling down the wall toward them! If only I had been capable of such feats back in Whitechapel I would never have had to leave at all. Perhaps I shall return one night, to continue my work. With my new gifts, I could no doubt work undisturbed, and undetected. These thoughts excite me, and I lick my lips.

I hunger.

And I must feed.

The first man's throat bursts open like a cracked egg between my jaws, hot blood erupting from the wound in steaming torrents. He drops his hand axe, not that it presented much of a threat to one such as I. I taste the metal of his blood and my entire body jolts with the power it gives me.

One of the others cries out in alarm. I slash his throat open with my fingernails, sharper and sturdier than any knife. He clutches at his neck as he goes down, his life's blood staining the front of his white shirt red. I leave him to expire at his leisure.

I feel a dull thud across my back. Another of the men looks in astonishment at the section of wooden plank that he holds in his hand. It has snapped in two.

Idiot.

To think he could harm me with such a puerile weapon.

I launch myself at him and snap his neck. He is dead before he hits the floor, his spinal cord twisted like rope.

I approach the fire where the last man cowers. He waves his hands at me, and begs. His words sound alien to me at first, and I realise he is speaking Romanian. Yet in an instant I find that I can understand his every pleading word! Another of my dark gifts has come to the fore. Whether it is due to my sisters' blood running through my veins, or the first henchman's sliding down my throat – or both! – I do not know. And I do not care. All I desire is to put an end to this man's futile prattling. I tell him to hush, not to worry, not to cry. Jack is here to sing him a sweet lullaby. I grip his idiotic face in my hand and smash the back of his head against the wall so hard that his brains, such as they are, smear across the stone surface. Then, tearing his collar away, I bare my fangs and lean in for the kill.

I will do this one slow.

And, oh, how I shall savour it.

CHAPTER TWENTY

The funereal sound of the ritualistic chanting had seemed to follow Mara all the way from the courtyard, a deathlike portent tolling in her ears. Try as she might, she still could not scrub the attendant spectacle of the hooded blood drinkers from her mind.

Yet her chance discovery of that ominous place and its grim secrets had put her, quite literally, back on the map. Unlike the poor Englishman, she had escaped from the courtyard unscathed. And now, by studying the map fragment at intervals, she had arrived at a door that she had not yet seen.

Mara steeled herself for what might lie beyond the door, and twisted its handle.

Warmth enveloped her as she opened the door and she saw the welcoming glow of a fire across the room. Satisfied that the room was unoccupied, she entered fully and slid the door shut behind her.

Mara did not need to refer to the map fragment to know where she was this time. The walls of the trophy room had become a gallery for stuffed animal heads and every surface was cluttered with a diverse selection of objects. A single wing-backed chair sat beneath an enormous stag's head complete with massive antlers that cast jagged, tree-branch shadows across the wall. Elsewhere, a stuffed boar grimaced in its death throes behind two vicious-looking tusks, and skulls of further conquests appeared to grit their teeth upon Mara's intrusion in their mausoleum. The mantelpiece above the hearth glimmered with the sheen from ornate picture frames and valuable trinkets that had been arranged there. The floor was dominated by a bear skin rug, complete with glass eyes. A cabinet that stood to one side of the rug seemed alive in the dancing light from candles that had been set into wall sconces around the room. As she neared the cabinet, Mara gasped in surprise to see a preserved head in a jar atop one of its shelves. The cranium of the specimen was distended, the dead features exaggerated by the curve of the preserving jar. The head's lifeless eyes gazed blankly at her, the orbs a filmy green colour due to the weird hue of the preserving fluid. Eager to turn her back on the sightless gaze of those unblinking eyes, Mara turned her attention to a sideboard stacked with rare tomes in a variety of languages. In front of the books, she found a leather bag, rather like a doctor's, which bore the initials "A.V.H.".

Intrigued, she opened the bag and found an odd array of items inside. A stethoscope's rubber tubing was entwined around the handle of a wooden mallet. Lifting the tangle from the bag revealed further items. A tobacco pouch, which she set aside next to the stethoscope and mallet, and a tiny Bible, written in Latin. Tucked inside its pages, Mara discovered a silver crucifix mounted on a slim chain.

Mara held the silver cross up to the candlelight, dazzling herself with its holy glow. She recalled a time when, as a mere child, she had gazed at a wooden cross, mounted on the wall above the fireplace in her father's house.

"Why do you hang a cross there, Dadda?" she had asked, and even now remembered his smile at his daughter's innocence.

"So that God may watch over us, always," he had said, before ruffling her hair as he always did when she interrupted him.

"Is that why people wear them around their necks?"

"Yes, my child, I suppose it is," he had told her.

Mara never had a crucifix to wear, as her father often struggled to put food on the table let alone indulge her with jewellery. Sometimes she climbed up on a stool and took the cross down from the wall. She would hold it up to the light until it made a shadow over her breast. If she could not wear a crucifix, then she would make sure that God's symbol fell upon her, even if only temporarily.

One day, the cross was gone, leaving only its faint outline in soot from the fire and the nails in the wall that usually held it in place. She wondered if the nails that the Village Fathers had told her once crucified Christ looked like them. Mara imagined they must have been much bigger to pierce all the way through a man's hand. The fire had almost died down by the time her father had returned home. She awoke to see him placing the cross back upon the wall.

"Where have you been with that?" she asked.

"To do God's will, child," her father had replied.

But if he thought that would be enough to placate her, he had been sorely mistaken. Mara quizzed him all the more as she ladled stew into his bowl, impatiently awaiting his answers in between each hungry mouthful.

Presently, his resolve diminished; no doubt because he knew he would get no rest until he told her where he had been. He explained that he and some of the villagers had been at the crossroads that night at the behest of the Holy Father.

"Do you recall I told you to keep away from the grazing meadows near the stream?" he asked her.

"I do recall, Dadda, and I swear I never set foot—"

"I know, child. You're a good girl. And you remember why I told you not to linger there?"

"Because a wild animal was attacking the poor cows. And the pigs. Oh, please tell me they are all right?"

"They are, now. We found what's been killing the livestock."

"What was it?" Mara had asked, spellbound.

"A *strigoi*," her father had said, "a vengeful spirit who, unhappy in life, had vowed to do others harm in death. And we villagers begged God to give us the strength to do something about it. The priest showed us the way."

"Will it not come back? Won't it be angry?" Mara had asked, fear permeating her every pore.

"Fear not, child. We removed its heart and then burned it. We stuffed the creature's mouth with garlic and then buried it at the crossroads. The Holy Father spoke scripture over it, and so you see, my child, there it will remain. If it were to awake someday, or night, it would remain stuck in the centre of the crossroads, uncertain which way to go and imprisoned in God's holy words.

"And you did all of this tonight, before supper?" she had asked incredulously.

He had simply nodded, before devouring the remainder of his meal, his tale told and done.

"I do not wish ever to be a grown-up!" Mara had said, weeping, and she must have said something funny for her father had laughed. Then he had embraced her, holding her tighter to him than ever before. And, even though he was laughing, she had felt tears fall from his eyes and into her hair.

Mara remembered, with a shiver, how not one soul from the village had ever again strayed near to the crossroads after dark, following the night her father told her his story.

Her thoughts now returning to her present situation, Mara looked at the glass eyes of the wall-mounted trophies gleaming golden in the firelight. She wondered what wild wonders God's creatures had witnessed in life, and what cruelty they had known in death. Brushing her hair to one side, she looped the chain around her neck and allowed the crucifix to hang over her heart.

Mara made a silent prayer that it would give her the strength to endure this night.

CHAPTER TWENTY-ONE

Grayson stumbled, battered, bruised and sore from his ordeal in the torture chamber, into the relative freedom of an adjoining corridor.

The inquisitor's words echoed in his already troubled mind ... *"You must atone. You must take the life of one of the other sinners ..."*

He winced at the pain in his thumbs as his hands found the hilts of the butcher's knives. His tortured digits felt five times their natural size after the pain that the inquisitor had inflicted upon them. Yet he had survived even that terrible ordeal, not to mention the vicious spikes of the iron maiden. He focused upon the knives, and their reassuring weight that pulled his belt lower beneath the overhang of his belly.

He had survived, and he was armed.

If there was to be only one guest left standing at the end of this most fateful night, he fully intended it to be him! At least the inquisitor's weapons would afford him some protection from whatever fell deeds the castle's denizens might prove themselves capable of.

He cycled back through his disjointed memories of his night in the castle thus far. The American had left him to his fate at the torturous hands of the inquisitor, but why hadn't he simply done away with him? Then he remembered the little glass vial the inquisitor had handed over to the American. Whatever its contents, they must have been precious indeed.

Poison, perhaps? A means by which to despatch a more sophisticated target? Maybe the cad meant to do away with Mara. He had seen the way the beast had looked at her aboard the train. His stark blue eyes had betrayed something deeper than mere dislike for the saucy little minx. Now Grayson thought of it, the American had regarded Mara with what could only be described as pure hatred. Grayson wondered if the poor girl still lived. She was a plucky sort. Perhaps the American would meet his match in one so well equipped with feminine wiles as she. It would certainly better the odds of survival for all of them if the Yank were to be eliminated from the running. Still, Grayson hoped he would never find out either way, for doing so would surely mean crossing paths with the terrifying American once more. The blighter's axe was larger even than his head, and that was saying something. No, better to avoid meeting the American at all, if possible.

He decided he would do well to stay out of reach of the stranger in the topper, also. A chap who wouldn't even show his face, let alone reveal his name, to his travelling companions might prove to be a force to be reckoned with in a tight spot. And there were tight spots aplenty in this cavernous old castle, with potential treachery at every turn! Grayson would have to try his luck with the easiest target, Lady Sophia, if he could only find her.

And then it came to him.

A eureka moment, of sorts.

Yes, Grayson recognised this bally corridor and the ornate doors a little way off from where he now trod. He was back in the corridor that had led to the great hall where he had dined – before Klove and his henchmen had executed the Russian. Grayson felt excitement bringing the colour back to his cheeks as he realised something else. He had seen the doorway through which Lady Sophia had been escorted by one of the burly attendants. All he had to do was to follow that trajectory and he might find the old dear's rooms. He gripped the handles of the butcher's knives as tightly as his ruined thumbs would allow and, with grim purpose, strode on toward the doors leading into the Great Hall.

***

He paused at the door and listened. Yes, he was getting better at this. Stealthy as a fox! Hearing nothing from inside, he reached out and turned the door handle before opening it just wide enough to peer inside. The room looked unoccupied. He stole inside and pulled the door closed behind him. The detritus of their earlier meal still lay untended upon the long table. How typically ill-mannered of Klove to have neglected to clear it away.

But Grayson felt a surge of gratitude after the fact when he saw, gleaming golden in the flickering light from the fireplace, the decanter of vintage port. He licked his lips. A restorative was exactly what he required, especially with the dread import of the inevitable task at hand. He crossed to the table and, finding a glass that looked to be unused, filled it to the brim with port. A mere two refills later, he was feeling much more like his bonny old self again. Now, which door was it that he had seen Lady Sophia go through after luncheon? He had felt sure she had left via the door adjacent to the fireplace but now he wasn't so sure. Perhaps another glass of port, to facilitate clarity of thought. Yes, a capital idea. He refilled the glass and lifted it to his eager lips and then saw light flickering in the doorway he had been considering. Powerful stuff, this port! And yet, the light flickered more intensely still. Grayson realised that someone must be approaching the door to the great hall and carrying a candle to light their way. His initial instinct was to hide, and yet the vast room seemed to offer no places in which to conceal himself. Under the table, perhaps? No, the table may be large but it was also narrow, and he would be seen. Behind one of the tapestries? He looked at the gap between the largest of them and concluded that his feet would be left exposed as they had been during many a round of hide and seek during his boarding school days. No, he was going to have to do something he rarely, if ever, did.

He was going to have to stand his ground.

In a moment, the door was flung wide and Grayson recoiled in fright as someone burst in carrying a lantern. Grayson could not quite make them out due to the brightness of the lantern light, and the angle at which it was being held. As his visitor held the lantern higher, Grayson saw revealed in its glow the inscrutable features of the same robed stranger whom he had witnessed tearing up the scroll of paper in an apparent fit of pique. He still struck Grayson as a queerly imposing figure, the gold thread decorating his robes sparkling in the light. Grayson thought it oddly flamboyant for a man who had refused to even introduce himself.

The lamp itself looked to be part of the castle, heavy and cast in iron. Its design was so aggressively Gothic that it seemed as though it had been fashioned from a portcullis. Its bearer paused for a moment at the edge of the room, glancing thereabouts as though searching for anyone who might be in hiding. Flamboyant, secretive, *and* paranoid. Quite the all-round misfit, this one, and a threat to boot.

Grayson watched him with growing curiosity as the fellow held the lamp steady and prowled into the room, in the manner of a great cat entering a cage for food. It was only when the stranger had reached the table that he seemed to become aware of Grayson. Perhaps exaggerated by the lamplight, Grayson noticed the intensity of the man's eyes. He possessed a wanderer's eyes, of a brownish hue so dark they could be mistaken for black, which only added to the alarming impression that this man had peered through the very Gates of Hell. Even now, as he set the lamp down upon the table, the light reflected in pinpricks from each eye pierced Grayson where he stood.

"I say, old boy, what do you say to a glass of port? It has warmed me up a little, and I ascertain from your garb that you perhaps hail from sunnier climbs, what?"

Those dark, pinprick eyes just stared back at Grayson and he began to feel uncomfortable beneath their gaze. It was as though the blighter was sizing him up.

"Rupert Grayson, Her Majesty's Rifles," he decided to offer.

Charm offensive. Yes, often the only way with this type of savage. A fellow spends too long scraping sand out of his beard and he begins to forget the social niceties. It was now up to Grayson to lead the way using his impeccable decorum. International relations seemed to stall, however, when the stranger stepped away from the table before muttering something unintelligible under his breath, and then spat on the floor. How uncouth! Grayson was dumbfounded for a moment, but then noticed something else other than the queer fellow's eyes twinkling in the lamplight. He had a golden blade tucked into a black and red sash belt that he wore slung around his waist. The blade was curved in the Eastern fashion, and the pommel shone ruby red with the jewel that crowned it.

The man had seen him looking at the weapon – had clocked his terror. Grayson quickly averted his eyes, making a show of pouring another glass of port.

"Well, old chum, if you're not game, perhaps I will—"

He was not afforded the opportunity to complete his sentence for, with a banshee-like wail, the sinewy stranger launched himself from aside the table, directly toward him. Time seemed to move slowly and it was as though the clock of Grayson's last moments on this earth was winding down. The sight of the man's golden blade, which he pulled from his sash belt with murderous intent, soon wound Grayson's clock again. Forgetting the butcher's knives in his own belt due to a sudden and cataclysmic onset of mortal panic, he reached for the most substantial object he could find.

The port decanter.

Grayson wielded it by its neck and felt its precious contents spill across his hand, stinging his sore thumb and trickling beneath the cuff at his wrist. It was reassuringly hefty in his hand and he – quite without thinking, for he was gripped now by a blind panic – sidestepped the approaching lunatic and swung it at the blighter's head with all the force he could muster.

There was a thudding crunch, and then the sound of something shattering. Whether it was the decanter breaking or the man's skull, Grayson did not know or care. The man faltered and fell, his momentum quashed by the mighty blow. Grayson heard what he thought was the roar of an appreciative crowd within his ears—

Bravo! Oh, good shot dear fellow! Down like a ninepin!

—only to realise a heartbeat later that it was the sound of his own panicked screaming. The decanter slid from his sweaty hand to the floor, where it certainly broke this time.

Grayson began to back away, his panic-stricken eyes fixed on the crumpled form of the man who lay before him.

Then, his worst nightmare.

He saw the man's hand twitch toward the golden blade. He was still conscious, and would no doubt be ever more intent on causing harm to Grayson's person! Grayson was rooted to the spot, heart in mouth and unable to move. Whereas his blow with the decanter had been delivered on instinct, his only instinct now was to run. But his feet would not budge.

He watched in abject terror as the man began to crawl to his blade. If he reached it, Grayson would be on the back foot – or on his back entirely! What he had seen in those eyes was the evil intent of a man who would kill to get what he wanted. Undoubtedly, he had nefarious designs upon Grayson's blood. The stranger, too, must have received dread instruction from their host to slay one of the other guests. He too must have been wandering the castle in search of easy pickings. How unfortunate for Grayson that he had timed his impromptu restorative with the arrival of this nasty-looking fellow. And oh, but now the rotter was mere inches away from the hilt of his fallen scimitar!

Grayson just simply had to act. But what to do? He was completely bloody petrified.

He closed his eyes momentarily and visualised a rugby ball instead of a golden scimitar. He imagined he was amidst the soil and sweat of the playing field at his old alma mater. A phantom breeze ruffled his thinning hair, and he fancied that he could hear the cries of his teammates, egging him on—

Go on Grayson, old fellow! Take the shot, dear boy! Give them what for, why don't you!

—to victory. He had never actually managed to score in those days, but needs must and all that. Grayson opened his eyes and focused on the target. Then he charged – a flat-footed, clod-hopping charge across the dining hall – but a charge all the same. With his last thundering stride, he took a great, sweeping kick—

Contact!

—the scimitar shot across the room and then rattled into the fireplace, kicking up a furnace of cinders. Again, the crowd roared in Grayson's ears, but he quickly realised once more, it was the sound of his own, bloodcurdling scream. While successfully disarming his opponent, he had smashed his toe against the golden scimitar by kicking the damnable thing. A spike of hot pain shot right up his leg from his toe, which had already begun to throb so hard he wondered if it was still attached to his foot. The intense, searing pain rivalled that of even the inquisitor's thumbscrews.

Without thinking, he lifted his injured foot to his hand and began hopping on the other while decorating the great hall with his choicest expletives. And it was at that very moment that his attacker made his move.

Grabbing hold of the ankle of the leg upon which Grayson stood, the stranger twisted it and then pulled with all his considerable might, toppling him over. Grayson's temple cracked painfully against the hard wooden edge of the banqueting table. He bit his tongue on impact, and tasted blood. Then, he spun round and felt the back of his head smack against the floorboards. If the floor had been stone he might be dead, or at the very least out for the count, Grayson realised through the harsh ringing in his ears.

He spat blood from his mouth and felt yet more trickling hot from the side of his head. With the blood came a fresh pang of panic for he heard his attacker muttering unintelligible curses of his own under his breath and feared that he meant this to be a fight to the death.

Grayson desperately wanted to move, but the dual impact to his head had him seeing stars. He felt like a man twice his age as he attempted to roll over and away from the stranger, who was now clawing his way across the floor toward him with a maniacal look in his eyes. Grayson saw for the first time the strange collection of jewelled rings on the fellow's fingers, and heard the jangling of metal hoops around his wrist. This chap had naught but trinkets, and yet the wild look in his eyes made Grayson believe him capable of murder with his bare hands. He looked unhinged, like a man possessed.

And then Grayson felt a reassuring presence at his side. The butcher's knives. They remained in harness at his waist. Fearing those bejewelled fingers as they groped toward him, Grayson freed one of the knives from his belt and slashed wildly out. The man screamed in aguish as the tip of the blade slashed through his right hand. The man recoiled, and tucked his bleeding hand under his arm.

"Back, you demon! Back!" Grayson implored, holding the knife out in front of him in dire warning. Its tip had tasted blood, and he hoped that was enough to send this maniac running.

He fumbled at his belt and took out the second butcher's knife, brandishing it at his opponent as menacingly as he could, given how bloody terrified he still was. It seemed to work because, as he did so, the wounded fellow got to his feet and staggered back a few steps. He leaned against the table, breathing heavily and clutching at his wounded hand.

Grayson glanced at the fireplace and saw the flames dancing around the golden scimitar. Safely out of bounds, and his opponent knew it too from the grim look on his face. Grayson's eye wandered then toward the nearest door, but the wounded man was blocking his way. Even without his curved blade, Grayson did not wish to be within an inch of this dubious sort ever again.

If he could only calm this fellow down a bit, even for a minute, then he might be able to make a run for it. Calling a truce seemed to be most noble remedy for this particularly sticky wicket. And so, with something of a flourish, he would be the first to admit, Grayson tucked first one, then the other butcher's knife back beneath the confines of his belt. He held up his empty hands in the manner of a huntsman to his hounds.

All gone! Down, boy!

The dark man squinted at him inscrutably, still clutching his damaged hand and allowing the table to support his weight against one hip. Then, without taking his eyes off Grayson, he straightened and stood to his full height before opening his wounded palm and pressing it down against the hot metal shell of the Gothic lantern atop the table. And oh, how the flesh of that hand sizzled! How awfully his blood spat! The fellow had obviously made some snap decision to cauterise the wound where he stood. If that was indeed his intent, why not pluck the scimitar from out of the fire? Surely that would do a capital job, and would grant the additional benefit of being armed once again. Grayson glanced to the fire, and then back at the stranger, whose pinprick eyes seemed to burn anew for each second he held his hand to the hot metal. His unwavering gaze was both a defiant taunt and a grave threat to Grayson. Those eyes seemed to say that any measure of inflicted pain could be endured – and returned in ample measure. Grayson found what little resolve he had at his disposal beginning to wither under the effects of that impenetrable gaze. His hands hung limp beside his sheathed butcher's knives; something about the man's gaze was making him feel rather queasy.

He swallowed, and then said, "Let's allow bygones to be bygones, what?"

The man removed his hand from the hot lamp. Grayson winced upon seeing steam rising from the man's flesh.

"Let us declare a truce. What do you say, old boy?"

The man took a deep inhalation of breath and, to Grayson's surprise, gripped his own shirt and tore it open, revealing dark, olive skin that was covered in tattoos. The ink described weird symbols and glyphs that seemed to have no beginning and no end as they overlapped every square inch of available skin. A disturbing thought came to Grayson. The symbols were remarkably similar to those he had seen engraved in the courtyard, directly before he had borne witness to the sinister ritual gathering held therein. The tattooed stranger lifted the Gothic lamp from the table and raised it high above his head.

"You devil!" Grayson exclaimed, quite beside himself as the man hurled the lamp at Grayson's feet.

In the next instant, flames sprang upwards, unleashed from the shattered glass of the lamp. Before he could react, Grayson's trousers had caught fire. After he'd patted at the flames on impulse, the cuffs of his jacket were alight too.

The tattooed man opened his mouth and the animalistic, guttural roar that issued forth struck new fear into Grayson's heart.

The sight of the devil advancing with that wild look etched into his eyes, the inked symbols undulating across his flesh as he powered toward him, gave Grayson cause to beat a hasty retreat.

Unfortunately, the only route that was open to him led to the window – the same window through which Rasputin had been flung into the moat.

Grayson knew the danger all too well. But he could also smell his own hair burning! The flesh below his knees was already stinging hot from the flames, his battered toe a nausea-inducing spike of pain as he put his weight upon it. He staggered and almost fell. The tattooed fiend was almost upon him. No time to spare. With the briefest inhalation of breath and a silent plea to Queen and country, Grayson spun around and hobbled, and then tumbled, toward the window.

CHAPTER TWENTY-TWO

Lady Sophia's thoughts took ever darker twists and turns as she tumbled into oblivion. A familiar face returned to her in the darkness, the face of a girl from long ago. And Lady Sophia remembered ...

The girl's name had been Elizabeth but she, rather commonly, preferred to be called Liza. It was a name known all too well to many a roughneck in the nearby village, although Lady Sophia had not discovered this fact until later in her servant's tenure. Much too late, as it had turned out. With the cruel advance of poor Archie's illness, Liza's duties had become focused almost entirely around his well-being. The girl claimed to have some nursing experience, gained by caring for a sick relative.

Perhaps weakened by the painful spectacle of Archie's deterioration, Lady Sophia had taken Liza at her word. It had proven to be a fatal mistake.

Lady Sophia had promised her husband that she would assist with commencement formalities at the university where he was a trustee, a commitment that meant a lengthy coach journey and an overnight stay. She had protested, of course, telling Archie that she would rather be at his side should he need her. But he had insisted, and so she had made the fateful journey, leaving Liza strict instructions to remain at his bedside for the duration, and to attend to his every need. The girl had duped her with affirmations that Archie would be in the safest of hands.

Because those hands, it would transpire, were far from safe at all.

She remembered how relieved she had felt when the carriage had rattled across the gravel to the front door of her home. Instead of staying over at lodgings, she had arranged for the driver to make the return journey immediately after supper. She had even managed to partake of forty winks during the journey. It was the early hours of the morning by the time she arrived, but at least now she would be back at her husband's side, where she was most needed, and where she truly belonged. And perhaps that shrewd sixth sense of hers had discerned that Liza's "safest hands" had been concealed behind her back the whole time she had conversed with her.

A giggle, coming from behind the rose bushes, had alerted her to the fact that something was amiss. Following the sound of the laughter she knew with dismay that it was Liza's even before she discovered the brazen girl lying with the groundskeeper on the croquet lawn. Clothes in scandalous disarray, and the ruffian clutching a crystal decanter of Archie's favoured single malt whisky, the two servants had laughed – actually laughed – when they saw her approaching across the lawn. Lady Sophia had given full vent to her fury, and only then did Liza seem to begin to realise the extent of her predicament.

Marching back to the house, Lady Sophia had found the front door open. An outrage! Any passing ne'er-do-well could have gained access to her home. Thieves could be ransacking the place while her poor, dear husband lay ill and vulnerable in his bed. And it had been to Archie's bedside that she had raced, driven on by phantasmagorical fears for his health. His room had been so quiet that she had heard the thump of her heartbeat as she rushed inside. The carafe of water by his bedside had toppled over, and she remembered seeing a dark circle of spilled water on the rug. She had righted the overturned carafe and perched gently on the side of his bed.

The dark circle of water was matched by that of his lifeless eyes. His mouth was fixed in a rictus of pain and terror. He lay there quite still, not breathing. Lady Sophia had vague memories of what happened next – events that seemed distant, like a dream half-remembered in that limbo state somewhere between sleep and waking.

Liza had sobbed and wailed, and protested her innocence. *"Sir was sound asleep, I swear! He was fine when I left him!"*

The groundskeeper had come indoors, swaying drunkenly in the hallway, still clutching that stolen crystal decanter in his filthy hand. Lady Sophia had demanded he hand it over. He had taunted her with insults, and had drained every last drop before handing it to her. His breath stank like a distillery as he laughed and mocked her. She used the decanter to stove his monstrous head in with a single, sharp blow to the temple. How Liza had screamed, all snot and tears at the sight of his blood pooling across the rug, until Lady Sophia had brandished the decanter at her. That shut the stupid girl up, for a while at least.

She had made the wretch help her drag the unconscious groundskeeper across the lawn where they had seen fit to lie together while her poor, dear Archie had died, alone and afraid.

It was fear of the workhouse, of never being able to live or work freely again, that had led the girl to help her mistress lift the groundskeeper over the lip of the well and down, down into its dark drop. Lady Sophia remembered feeling cool and calm, almost serene, as she had chained the girl up beside the well. The wretch could watch her lover wake, and then die slowly from his injuries at the bottom of the well.

It took several days, and long nights, until he expired, underscored by a symphony of Liza's cries and wails. Then, those too expired, and Lady Sophia had unchained the girl and offered her the choice of a lifetime of servitude in her household, or else to join her former lover in an ignominious death.

Lady Sophia remembered the cracking sound that Liza's bones had made when they had broken at the bottom of the well. She had felt nothing when the girl had thrown herself in, only the deep remorse that she would never see Archibald alive again. She would have to tell him how she had avenged him when they were reunited in the family mausoleum, and in the hereafter.

She saw once again, in her mind's eye, the dark circle of spilled water on the rug beside her poor, dear Archie's bedside. The circle became the well into which the evil lovers had met their end. Her memories drifted away. And then, she opened her eyes and saw circles within circles. Her vision was so blurry.

She blinked, and tried to focus.

A faint outline coalesced, high above her. It was the hole in the wall. It seemed so very far away. A mere pinprick of light in a vast ocean of black. As her eyes struggled to focus in the semi-darkness, her other senses began to return to her, bringing with them the dull ache of pain. She saw the yellow-blue flame of the torch, sputtering where it had fallen on the stone floor. Weird shapes moved in the gloom, against the curved walls of the vertiginous abyss into which she had been so cruelly pushed. And after she had attempted to save the girl-child! This ruination, this utter degradation, was to be her thanks? A cold tear trickled down her face. It could not end like this. Not for her! Yet she could not move her arms or legs. Could not even feel her fingers, her toes.

She ground her teeth together as she forced her hand to move, but as she did so a sharp spike of pain rattled through her legs and arms, shocking her heart into palpitations. With a trembling hand, she moved her hand across the wet, stony floor. Her fingertips touched something soft and wet. She probed yet further and felt the jagged bone of a compound fracture poking through ravaged flesh. It was her own leg, she realised in terror and dismay, folded back on itself. The realisation awakened her shattered nerve endings and she gasped and then wailed in agony. Her voice echoed around her in the claustrophobic space before breaking off, fragile in the punishing maelstrom of her pain.

Broken and bleeding, she felt the last of her strength depart her body. Her hand fell limp to the floor and there it remained. She willed her fingers to move, to somehow reach out and drag the flickering torch closer to her that she might enjoy its diminishing warmth in her final moments. For she knew that the end was near.

She knew she must remain brave to the last. She would be reunited with her beloved, she had to believe that. He would be waiting for her, to lead her to Paradise!

The flame flickered and sizzled against wet stone. She whimpered in abject fear. A single pair of red eyes was watching her intently from the shadows. The torch flame fizzled and popped, about to flicker its last.

As it died, she saw hundreds of those red eyes, fierce as hot coals, and the last of her bravery was extinguished within her. She knew she was alone, and so far away from her beloved. He was at rest in the family tomb. No one would know where she lay. No one would care. Her Archie would remain apart from her for all eternity.

Heralding the sudden darkness, the screeches of a legion of rats erupted all around her. They closed in, their monstrous, slimy bodies wriggling eagerly over her body. She felt their razor-sharp teeth biting and gnawing at her flesh.

Lady Sophia's final, terrified screams of despair became her epitaph in the fathomless dark of the oubliette.

CHAPTER TWENTY-THREE

The glass shattered around Grayson as he propelled himself through the window and into night's void.

Wisps of smoke blurred across his vision as he spiralled. He could not tell if the fall was putting the flames out, or fanning them. Cold air shocked him alert and, falling backwards now, he looked up. Grayson saw the tortured visage of his attacker as it emerged through the broken window, those pinprick eyes watching him fall. On and on he plummeted, a human torch lighting up the night sky on his descent.

There came an explosion of noise around him as he hit the surface of the moat. The water quenched the flames in an instant. Momentum had slammed him beneath the water and gravity was now sinking him deeper beneath its surface. He began moving his arms and legs to slow his descent, tiny air bubbles escaping from his lips in the murky black water.

Desperate to get to the surface to take a precious breath of oxygen, he kicked out his feet beneath him and felt a sickening jolt of pain at the base of his damaged big toe. He struggled upwards, the tattered remnants of his trousers trailing behind him like waterweeds, until he saw pale, white moonlight above like a flag beckoning him to a finish line.

Almost there. Almost at the surface.

Then, he felt a disturbance in the water beneath him. The sensation was rather like being on a rope bridge, elevated by some unseen air current. The movement propelled him further toward the surface, but after it had passed, he felt himself dragged back down in its wake. Something enormous had passed directly beneath him in the depths of the moat.

Before he could ascertain what the thing was, Grayson felt its unwelcome return. He tried to right himself as the water churned and roiled all around him, the sudden undulation pulling him under. He fought his way back to the surface and gulped in a lungful of precious air before the sideward current sucked him under again. He grimaced at the sensation as a mouthful of cold, dirty moat water lapped at his throat. Grayson paddled wildly, course-correcting against another great, roiling wave. He fought hard to avoid becoming ensnared within its vortex and, as he righted himself, he saw tantalising flashes in the moonlight of the muddy bank on the moat's outer edge.

Gripped by an urgent, increasing panic, he swam frantically for the bank. Grayson clawed at the water like a lunatic, head down, legs scissoring as fast as he could move them. All the while, he could feel the presence of the unseen thing in the water at his feet. He willed himself on, taking a quick lungful of air before cutting faster through the water.

The tips of his fingers brushed against the muddy bank. His knees brushed the slope where it met the water. Grayson dug his fingers into wet clay, his tortured thumbs protesting as he began to crawl onto solid, if slippery, ground.

He had bally well made it!

Then he felt the water lapping at his calves and heard a slithering sound as something coiled around his ankle and dragged him, at terrifying speed, back down into the moat. His relief was knocked out of him, along with his breath. The pressure of its vice-like grip around his ankle was matched only by the harsh stinging sensation he felt at its touch. Eyes bulging in panic in the dark water, he now felt row upon row of sickly grey suckers lining the length of this cold, muscular protrusion. He rolled over in the water and glimpsed his nemesis. A massive tentacle had latched onto him with its foul stingers!

Grayson gritted his teeth against the intense pain caused by those stingers, trying not to open his mouth and let the last of his vital oxygen escape. The tentacle dragged him powerfully away from the castle wall, toward the centre of the moat and deeper into the darkness. He felt another tentacle coil around his waist, squeezing more breath from his body, the suckers wounding his flesh through his clothes. Another gripped his wrist and he was powerless to resist it. Helpless, he rolled over, guided inexorably by the tentacle – toward whatever nightmare it was attached to.

As he gaped in mortal terror, he saw only blackness below. Just how deep must the moat be to contain such a monstrous thing! The tentacles rolled him over and through the water as effortlessly as a spider manipulating prey into her web.

For a split second, the moonlight that barely penetrated the surface of the moat revealed something there in the blackness – an enormous, lidless, eye, its aspect entirely alien and without conscience. In that split second, Grayson saw the distorted mirror image of his own face at the centre of that unblinking eye. The curved black surface was as unyielding as onyx and, as the tentacles pulled him closer to it, the effect was that of gazing into a huge scrying mirror and seeing only his own futile reflection.

All went black once more and Grayson felt movement. A leviathan stirring in the water. It was as though an entire world was uncoiling, flexing beneath him, and displacing the entirety of the water in the moat as though it were a mere rain puddle. Grayson struggled against the tentacles but the more he did so, the tighter they coiled. This must have been the Russian's lonely fate, he thought in anguish, but whereas the holy man must have had prayers to ease his passage to the hereafter, Grayson only had silent screams of terror.

The leviathan's maw opened, sending the sounds of a chorus of dying children through the water. Grayson ground his teeth as the cacophony assaulted his eardrums with unbearable pressure. The vibration hummed through every fibre of his being, a dark song from which there was no escape.

Nor was there any hope of escape from what came next, for he felt a tunnel-like mouth lined with endless spirals of lethal curved and spiny teeth all about him. The tentacles tightened around his body, their stingers gouging deeper into his flesh as they pulled him in to that monstrous cake-hole at a frightening pace.

He was fish food, and that was that.

He wriggled, kicked, and thrashed against the constraints of the tentacles. The suckers around his ankle held tight, but he managed to free his wrist when his shirtsleeve tore away.

This was his chance. Perhaps his *only* chance!

Grabbing one of the butcher's knives, he slashed wildly at the tentacle coiled around his ankle. He grimaced in agony at the sucker stings on his skin as he wrenched his leg away from the tentacle. Foul fluid seeped into the water and up his nostrils as the tentacle recoiled from the knife wound. Almost losing his grip on the butcher's knife, he quickly liberated the other from his belt.

Kicking forward in the water, he held one knife blade in front of him like a bayonet and felt it plunge into something soft. Cold, alien jelly erupted around his fist and he knew that he had penetrated that awful lidless eye. A hideous cloud of inky blood filled the water around him, the nightmare rot and ruin of whatever foulness had spawned this disgusting denizen of the deep. A vicious tentacle lashed out, stinging his face before coiling around his neck, a living death noose.

He slashed out with the other knife, cutting clean through the tentacle and releasing yet more foul effluent. The creature howled – a noise like the world ending – and then tumbled repeatedly in the depths. One of his knives wrenched away from his hand, buried hilt-deep in the eldritch thing's eye. Grayson hoped that if a brain lurked somewhere beyond that disgusting sphere of jelly, his blade had pierced it. He fancied it had because the creature rolled over like a wounded manatee, corkscrewing back through the water. Grayson hacked and slashed at its gargantuan slimy body and the lethal tentacles that still thrashed around him in the water. Then, he kicked away from the beast and swam for all he was worth.

He broke the surface, gasping in pain, but did not dare pause to look behind him. Even though his lungs were screaming for respite, it was only when he neared the castle wall that he allowed himself a moment's pause. Carried by a strange current that was sweeping him ever further from the mud bank, he glanced across the moonlit surface of the moat. It was once more still and calm in his wake, as though the monstrous beast that dwelled there was nothing but a figment of his tortured imagination. Yet his heart still beat a tattoo of terror, and his flesh still burned from the branding iron grip of those evil tentacles. Even now, with lingering terror, did he expect to see them break the surface and drag him to his murky doom.

Motivated by these terrors, Grayson kept close to the castle wall, and swam with the current. Hope was renewed within him when he saw that a section of wall had crumbled away from disrepair. Thick vines of ivy and creeper had taken root in the exposed mortar. Grayson swam for a stout root that was drooping into the black water and grabbed hold of it. His arms shook from pain and exhaustion as he attempted to scramble up the vine. His drenched clothing was making him even heavier, and the vine gave way, soil and dust raining down on him from the decrepit mortar that was barely holding the castle wall together.

He fell back into the moat with an ungodly splash and swallowed yet more foul and freezing water. He surfaced and began to tread water, all the while feeling exhaustion taking hold. Shivering from the cold, a sense of all-pervading dread began to sap the last of Grayson's strength. He must climb out, or he would surely drown! Spitting the last of the horrid water back into the moat, he saw the leaves of a thicker vine gleaming wetly in the moonlight, just inches above the moat's surface.

Using his remaining butcher's knife as a climbing tool, and knotted sections of vine and ivy as hand and footholds, he dragged his soggy bulk inch by inch up the crumbling wall. Fragments of brick and mortar splashed into the water below and his fear reached fever pitch as he imagined other tentacled creatures of the deep surfacing to ensnare him, attracted by the noise. The fingers of his free hand found purchase on a morass of roots nestled in the brickwork and he pulled himself up. Reaching the topmost row of loose bricks, he tumbled clumsily over them as the entire remaining section of wall gave way. His butcher's knife slipped from his hand and followed the avalanche of bricks into the moat.

Grayson then rolled over onto bare soil, his lungs at breaking point, his body a numb and knotted tangle. He blinked at the blurred canopy of stars that twinkled through the overhanging branches of tall trees and tried to control his breathing. Yet, as the adrenaline receded and the cold sharpened his senses, he felt only pain. Terrible, all-consuming pain. His arms, legs and torso were red raw with dozens of angry circles where the tentacles had stung him, livid puncture wounds oozing blood at the centre of each. As the cold air bit into his flesh like phantom teeth he realised he could no longer move his thumbs. The damage the inquisitor's thumbscrews inflicted had increased tenfold as a result of his desperate fight in the moat. He rolled over and tried to get to his feet. Grayson cried out in agony as he felt his big toe dangling and broken inside what was left of his shoe. His legs buckled uselessly and he toppled over headfirst into the dirt.

He lay there in agony for some time, shivering in shock at his wounds and from the icy cold. Only then did he take in his surroundings and realise where his desperate flight had delivered him. For it was not only tree branches that cast their shadow over him here. In all directions, for as far as his eyes could see from his lowly vantage point in the dirt, stood row upon row of headstones.

He was in a graveyard.

"What did I do in a previous life to deserve this fate!?" Grayson cried out in anguish.

As cold tears poured from his eyes, the very light of the stars above seemed to melt away and vanish, casting him into utter darkness.

CHAPTER TWENTY-FOUR

The nameless wanderer winced at the pain in his right hand. The lamp had cauterised the wound, but it had cut deep beneath his flesh. He did not need his memory to know that this castle was a place of great evil, and its inhabitants meant him only harm. Enraged, he had watched the pink-skinned man swimming to the bank of the moat far below in the moonlight. His attacker was weakened, and the wanderer now meant to finish what he had started. He set off in the rough direction of his assailant and soon found a staircase leading into the very guts of the castle. Without a lantern, he had clawed his way through the dark, his bare hands guiding him along raven-black passageways until he reached a wooden door.

He smashed the door open with his fists, careless of the pain he felt at his extremities, and strode out into the open air. Cold starlight revealed that he was standing on a stone path that wound away from the castle and into a tree-lined cemetery.

How apt that a thoughtless revenant such as he should find himself in the home of the dead!

As he walked on, he noticed that the cold night air was making gooseflesh of his tattooed skin, the only indication that he was a living thing in this desolate outdoor mausoleum.

He continued until he reached an open grave, its sheer sides a tangle of roots, soil, and stones. The smell of freshly dug earth was as a balm to him, inviting him to lie down upon its bed, never to rise again.

Movement startled him, and he realised that he was not the only living thing in this morbid place after all. The flickering glow of an oil lamp revealed the silhouette of a gravedigger who toiled a short distance away. The man was digging another grave with a rusty metal shovel, his back bent from decades of such exertions.

He would require a lamp to light his way. After all, he had smashed his first at the feet of his attacker in the great hall. The gravedigger's would do, he decided. He wandered over to the mound of earth where the lamp now lay and reached for it with his good hand.

The gravedigger, coughing and wheezing, whirled around in his filthy hole and cried out in protest. He muttered a string of local expletives and then, apparently afraid of the look he found in his visitor's eyes, held up his hands in surrender.

Taking the lamp, the wanderer withdrew and decided to see where the winding path led. He was about to follow it between the headstones when he heard the gravedigger laugh. The wheezy cackle echoed mockingly around the cemetery. The wanderer turned back, but the old man had already gone, leaving the open grave unattended. The wanderer held the lamp aloft. The grave was lined with chalky, tooth-like rocks that made it look disturbingly like a mocking mouth in the half-light. The wind whistled icily through the bare branches of the tree, trailing serpentine shadows on the ground. How such a decrepit, hunchbacked old gravedigger could move so fast was yet another mystery to add to his catalogue. The wanderer directed the light of his requisitioned lamp this way and that but could see no one at all.

The path led him into the thick of the cemetery, where headstones and statues crowded the area, as densely packed as trees in a wild forest. He heard the gravedigger's laughter again, and hoped it was just an echo in his imagination. But with each step he took the laughter increased in volume, making his brain reel as though from some internal head injury. On and on the laughter went, shredding the last vestiges of his sanity until the ground seemed to tilt beneath him. He lost his footing and staggered straight into a tomb.

He fell against the structure, winded, cursing and raging. At last, the gravedigger's mocking laughter ceased, snuffed out on the wind that whispered through the bare branches of the trees. Those trees stood silently watching from beyond the rows of the buried in this deathly place.

He steadied himself against the white marble surface of the tomb using the flat of his wounded hand. The cold marble soothed his stinging flesh. His fingers explored the structure, so perfectly smooth, until they found an inscription chiselled there. He read the epitaph and, in an instant, the floodgates of his mind burst open.

Memories began to return to him, a steady trickle of remembrance that quickly became a torrent of not only sights, sounds, and other base sensations, but of places, and names. An entire human history thundered into his consciousness with all the ferocity of a tsunami. In the maelstrom, he witnessed the threads of his life's path knitting together … backwards through time … beneath skies both earthly and alien … to the dark epicentre of his soul … and of who he truly was.

***

His calling had taken him to cities far from his humble desert beginnings, away from the bosom of his mother and the nomads that were his extended family. For, one night as a boy, he had chanced upon a spirit in the desert that spoke to him from the flames of a burning tree. The spirit had awakened a higher purpose within him, and set him upon his ritual path to enlightenment. He wandered for ten years and then ten more in pursuit of the knowledge that would allow him to reach his true potential. Forbidden knowledge to those whose weakness would rob them of faith and give them cause to question it, but not he. He began to inscribe his accumulation of mysteries into a book that he carried with him at his breast. Into this book he poured secrets heard scattered on the four winds, ritual workings chanted in the darkest, hidden places of the earth, all of them blessings bestowed upon him by those with whom he alone communed.

His final ritual was to last seven months, seven weeks and seven days, culminating under a constellation that appeared only once in millennia. He remembered seeing his wife's eyes in the bazaar and, seeing them glitter like jewels, even feeling a little saddened at the prospect of what he must do. Yet do this he must, if he were to reach the full enlightenment to which he had devoted a lifetime.

He had proposed to her without any recourse to her father for he had passed some time ago. His betrothed's mother was glad of the coin he offered as dowry. And, no sooner were they wed, than he had whisked his bride away beneath a honey-coloured moon. And into the desert.

They travelled as nomads in the manner of his forebears. By day they followed the sun, and at night he transcribed the language of the stars into his notebook. He had promised his wife an adventure and, during the sandstorms that frequented their secret pathways into the desert, she cleaved to him in the night and he felt virile and powerful. Yet the real power was yet to come.

At last, he found the place where two mountains met, just as the spirits had instructed him. Leaving their camels behind, he packed up what little they required for the final leg of their journey. He then led his wife by the hand into a place as yet unseen by human eyes, the nameless city where boundless riches awaited them. Never again would she want for anything, never would she have to feel the shame of having stolen bread from the market simply in order to survive. She hung upon his every word as though each were a golden thread, weaving together her destiny.

The deserted city was a place of awe-inspiring wonder. The sheer size and geometry of its construction seemed beyond the workings of human mind, or hand, and yet there it stood, an indomitable testament to a long-forgotten civilisation.

The sun was going down by the time they had traversed the endless city streets in search of the opening to a legendary temple. After a brief period of rest, during which he waited for the stars to align in the heavens above, he led her by torchlight into the tunnels beneath the city. The tunnels formed a vast network that only he possessed the insight to navigate. They soon came upon a sunken chamber at the place where the tunnels met. Its cathedral-sized walls were lined with eldritch carvings of creatures too alien to describe. Yet, even as his enthusiasm took hold, his wife had begun to show fear at what they had found in that subterranean place.

He had known then that it was time.

Allaying her fears with reminders of the riches that would soon be theirs, he led her on until they reached two enormous golden gates, taller than the minarets of home. Holding his flaming torch aloft, they gasped in unison at the wondrous sight beyond. An entire underground city sprawled, several times larger than that which stood above them. Towers and bridges seemed to sprout from the very rock, their surfaces shimmering with an otherworldly, incandescent light. He heard voices whispering from within, directing him in ancient tongues toward his true and final enlightenment.

He turned to his wife, ritual dagger unsheathed, for he knew the attainment of such forbidden knowledge bore the ultimate price, and that its currency was of flesh and blood. Those beautiful eyes had widened in astonished innocence as he took the living light from them as an offering to the ancients. Where he had once promised the consummation of their love, he now condemned his beloved to an eternity of damnation.

As she lay bleeding, the gates had opened for him with a metallic clank that rang out throughout the cavernous space like the pealing of church bells. The Old Ones had accepted his offering of flesh and blood, and had beckoned him into their realm.

Hours, days, aeons had passed within a span of minutes. Time became meaningless, seeming to stretch and then reconfigure, as did his mind, which fractured and healed, over and over without end, as he received their forbidden knowledge. He transcribed their secrets into his book so feverishly that his fingertips began to bleed, his blood merging with the ink on the page, before becoming the ink. When he ran out of pages, he tattooed the secrets into his skin, fusing his very being with the dark knowledge that surged through his most precious book, his *Al Azif.* He no longer knew nor cared where the pages ended and he began. He was an extension of the book, as voracious as an inexhaustible well, the secrets within him as fathomless as all the darkness in the universe.

***

He blinked away his memories and gazed once more at the name inscribed upon the marble tomb:

Here lies Abdul Alhazred

And beneath it, read:

That is not dead which can eternal lie,
And with strange aeons even death may die

He was a wanderer, yet nameless no more. For, in that instant, he knew that he had found his own name upon the marble tomb in the cemetery of this accursed castle!

Then, he heard a shuffling sound from between the graves. Peering into the distance, seeing as though through new eyes, he spied someone crawling through the ground fog toward him, unaware of his presence.

Alhazred clenched his fists and felt his mind and body tingle with the first stirrings of the dark power that was returning to him.

CHAPTER TWENTY-FIVE

Grayson panted, cold sweat pouring down into his eyes as he crawled through the graveyard and toward the castle. Twisted trees cast their sinister shadows over lichen-covered gravestones and tumbledown tombs, which dotted the fogbound landscape all around him.

The pain from his broken toe made him gag with nausea and his ruined thumbs seemed to scream in protest with his every move. He paused for breath, his moat-sodden lungs rattling weakly, the cloud of vapour from his lips mingling with that of the ground mist through which he crawled.

Glancing back over his shoulder, he saw with dismay that he had only managed to crawl twenty feet or so. Such a short distance in what felt to his battered and punctured body and half-drowned lungs to have taken hours! Grayson's teeth began to chatter at the chill air turning his wet clothing into a shroud of cold fear that penetrated his very bones. How he longed to be away from this morbid place, and beside a roaring fire! He resigned himself to the long and painful crawl back to the castle. Groaning in agony as he pulled himself onward, he spied a dark shape up ahead. It was a door in the outer wall, just visible through the shifting curtain of chill mist. His salvation! To reach it, he had only to cross a short wooden bridge that spanned a babbling brook which, by the looks of things, fed the foul moat with ice-cold water from the mountains.

He crawled on, gritting his teeth against the pain from his myriad injuries, across a patch of boggy, uneven ground. He could now make out the outline of a structure that no longer stood beside the mountain wall. The stone foundation described the layout of a small outbuilding, a chapel perhaps, and Grayson remembered how the bricks within the crumbling wall of the old jetty had a similar hue. As he neared the low bricks where sturdy walls once stood, he spied a font at their centre. The white marble had turned moss green from exposure to the elements. Ivy grew up the font's pillar, and into its basin, where stagnant water sat in place of the holy water it would once have contained. What kind of God-fearing man would tear down a chapel with which to repair his outer wall?

A man who did not fear God at all, thought Grayson with a shudder.

Grayson dragged himself up to the bridge and, grasping its rickety wooden handrail, pulled himself up and onto one foot. As he hopped and squelched his way over the bridge to the other side, Grayson tried placing a little weight on his damaged foot and regretted it in an instant. His brain flashed white with a lightning bolt of pain that shot from his fractured toe and up through his body. Falling to his knees and crawling like a dog, Grayson was then surprised to see, between the gravestones, a yellow glow coming from the other side of a thick-trunked tree. He crawled toward the light, a moth to a flame, and saw a dark figure holding a hurricane lantern and peering straight at him through the mist! Grayson recognised the brute in an instant. Those mad eyes, that crazed snarl, and above all else the blasphemous pictograms inked into the flesh of his exposed chest and arms.

It was the same tattooed wanderer he had fought in the great hall.

Grayson reached for the knife that was no longer there. Hellfire and damnation, he had lost his last line of defence to the moat!

The tattooed man strode toward him across the cemetery, and Grayson noticed with alarm that the fellow's gait had changed entirely. He looked no longer to be the wild, twitchy man he had encountered in the hall, but rather strident. As he approached, his grim visage lit by the yellow glow of the hurricane lamp, Grayson felt more afraid than ever of this man. He looked taller somehow, and not just because Grayson was on his hands and knees. The man's lithe movements between the tombstones were almost effortless, his sinewy body seeming to pulse with an inner strength.

Grayson crawled backwards, away from the tattooed madman, and cried out in alarm as he almost plunged into the mouth of an open grave. It was too late, he had nowhere left to crawl, and the tattooed man was upon him in an instant.

The man reached down and clamped the fingers of his free hand onto Grayson's forehead. The cad's fingers were like claws, bone hard, and it felt as though they were burrowing into his skull. Grayson cried out in agony as he felt himself dragged from the edge of the grave and into a kneeling position on the ground, his head held fast by those painfully pointy fingers.

Then, the man uttered a few words in some ancient, obscure tongue. A wave of freezing cold darkness gripped Grayson's brain, turning it to ice inside his skull. A psychic blast shot from the tips of the tattooed man's fingers and uncoiled into the very privations of his brain. Grayson's vision turned frighteningly red.

And then, his mind shattered.

He felt those fingertips release him, but he carried their touch inside his skull as he groped between the gravestones, dragging his damaged foot behind him . He blinked the redness away until his vision cleared, yet all seemed dark and indistinct around him. He staggered blindly away, picturing the door to the castle but finding only confusion. The cemetery had become a battlefield, the graves were turned to trenches, the tree branches now tangles of barbed wire.

A terrible ringing in his ears gave way to the aural assault of past conflicts. Grayson clamped his hands over his ears in a futile attempt to blot out the noise of staccato gunfire, the whine of artillery shells, and the screams of men torn asunder by the ensuing blasts. Grayson staggered through the chaos, attempting to escape the cacophony that raged inside his head, but it only grew more intense with each tenuous step across the uneven ground. He stumbled and fell to his knees once more. Just inches from his face stood a makeshift grave marker in the shape of a cross formed of two planks from a trench. His eyes found their focus, taking in the letters etched there. A name.

Baker. He had known a Baker during his first campaign. Poor blighter hadn't made it beyond the first day of action. Gritting his teeth, Grayson saw other names on more wooden crosses around him: *Edwards, Sullivan, Baldock, Warren, Campbell-Sinclair* … All of them were achingly familiar to him. These were the epitaphs of the war dead, those among the legions he had deserted in order to save his own skin. Row upon row of their names faced him now, their forgotten monikers forming ranks of accusation against him.

Grayson screamed in terror as something burst from the soil in front of the nearest war grave: a gnarled, grey hand that clawed at the chill night air like a dying weed seeking sunlight. The horribly ragged fingernails of the hand were encrusted with dirt, the veins beneath the skin a deathly blue colour. Another hand emerged from the earth, followed by a body. Grave worms slithered in the folds of the cadaver's rotting uniform as it crawled into view.

The soldier's face was as pale as moon glow, his eyes blind blobs of jelly in the putrefaction of his decaying eye sockets, which writhed with maggots. His mouth opened in a sick approximation of a smile and loose, blackened teeth dislodged as his disgusting tongue lolled over his dead lips. A deathly stench emanated from the soldier's cadaverous lungs, making Grayson recoil in revulsion.

He staggered away and was stopped in his tracks by what he saw next. Dozens more dead soldiers were rising from their graves, their uniforms in rotten and bloody tatters. Some had missing limbs and so crawled out and onto the ground. Others had lost their eyes, or even entire sections of their skulls. Yet still they moved, their dead organs visible and glistening in a terrifying mockery of life everlasting. This hideous, un-living and yet mobile battalion of the dead shuffled into ranks. He gasped in abject terror as he saw them marching toward him, each exhaling the foul, bitter stench of the grave.

Grayson shrieked in terror and limped away between the grave markers, skirting the clawing hands of more soldiers emerging from what should have been their resting places. Propelled by pure dread, he staggered on through the fog of the battlefield. He could see the vague outline of a door up ahead. He glanced back at the undead soldiers shuffling along behind him. By gad, there were hundreds! He turned his attention back to the door – and tumbled headlong into a lethal coil of barbed wire.

He screamed as the barbs bit into his tender flesh. Roaring in agony as the barbs tore through the meat of him, he felt hot blood spurt from fresh wounds in his belly and knees. Beside him, trapped in the wire, he saw a severed hand, the skin shredded away to reveal the workings of the bones beneath. The hand moved, and terror propelled him on. He crawled toward the door, desperate to be free of the wire and away from that ghastly, reanimated hand. His blurry eyes fixed upon a chink of light that glowed from within like a beacon of hope.

Grayson crawled inside and, with his one good foot, slammed the door behind him. He was inside a narrow stone stairwell that led upwards, back into the castle. Leaning against the wall, with his trembling hand he pulled himself erect and saw drops of his blood coating the bottom step. As he took his first, painful step aloft, he heard hundreds of dead hands scratching at the door behind him.

CHAPTER TWENTY-SIX

Abdul Alhazred watched the Englishman stagger away across the graveyard, savouring his wild screams of terror as though they were a beautiful symphony.

And he knew they were yet to reach their crescendo for his mad visions would penetrate ever deeper into the man's shallow, tiny mind before his end.

Let him succumb to the darkness of who he really is, Alhazred thought, *for only in the darkness may we finally know our truth.*

Ignoring the man's howls of terror for the moment, Alhazred's gaze fell upon a pitchfork that leant against the trunk of a tree overhanging the open grave. The gravedigger had left it behind, no doubt. He walked over to it, reached down, and picked it up. It seemed sturdy enough, the prongs were still intact and their tips looked sharply lethal after he brushed away the mud that coated them. He swung it through the air and those metal prongs whistled in the night air. More music to his ears.

A grim smile curled the corners of his mouth as he saw the Englishman stagger and then fall once more. It seemed that whatever visions he had conjured were taking hold, for the man was wailing and thrashing about in terror, as though against some unseen foe.

Alhazred breathed in the cool, crisp air, his senses born anew following his reawakening. In an instant, his fingers found his precious, most holy book in the folds of his robes. His life's work. His *Al Azif*. His *Necronomicon*. He closed his eyes in silent prayer for a moment and heard an echo of The Old One's voice. It reverberated across time and space from the subterranean desert chamber of his deliverance and into his very soul. Yog Sothoth's voice was as sonorously beautiful as it had been then, when he had first heeded its call. Its recitations were an eldritch litany that sounded like all the sanity of the world being crushed beneath an enormous, cloven hoof. And with the litany, once again, came power. More power than even he could contain.

Every vein, every synapse within him, now crackled and surged with limitless, dark energy. His was a force that could uproot entire forests, roll back oceans, and level mountains. He would rule in the elder gods' stead, until they returned through him. Summer's fire would come to burn away amnesia's long winter, to feast upon a limitless harvest of flesh, blood, and bone. The machinery of man's destruction turned like cogs within his black heart. He was their angel, their death, and their saviour.

Gripping the pitchfork as though it were a trident, he strode after the Englishman. He would tear this castle apart, brick by brick, until all that remained was dust.

CHAPTER TWENTY-SEVEN

I f only Mara had within her possession the remainder of the map! She had strayed beyond the perimeter of the fragment that she had found tucked inside the journal and become lost once again in the castle's maze-like passageways.

The journal ... Of course ...

Castigating herself for not thinking of it sooner, Mara pulled the book from her clothing and began leafing through its pages, hoping against hope that her hunch might be proven right. She paused at a page containing one of the maps that had caught her eye earlier. The page had been torn away at an angle so that a portion of its map was missing. With a trembling hand, she placed her fragment beside the missing part of the torn page. It fit almost perfectly! Mara moved her candle closer to the page in order to study the map, now that she had made it whole again.

It depicted a bridge and the floorplan of a structure, undoubtedly the castle in which she stood. The mapmaker had rendered the circular shape of a tower at the north-eastern edge of the floorplan, and it looked to be accessible by only one route. Mara recalled the ominous instruction from the note left in her boudoir about bringing some proof of having slayed one of the other guests to the tower. Such a tower might offer the most defensible situation in the entire castle, and yet the invitation to bring such grisly proof to the very same location made it anathema to her. Checking the position of the moon in the sky, and then seeing Orion's belt twinkling like diamonds on a necklace against night's black velvet, she knew exactly which direction led to the tower. Mara turned round and began walking back the other way.

And then she saw a figure in the shadows.

She held her candle aloft, but it was too dark in the distant passageway to see his features clearly. He moved with an awkward, lumbering gait, and Mara noticed he was dragging one leg along behind him. As he drew nearer, she heard him coughing and muttering under his breath, a stream of gobbledegook. Periodically he stopped and turned before waving his arms around wildly, as though warding off invisible phantoms. Moonlight from the archway revealed that the man was covered from head to toe in blood, his clothing in tatters. He shuffled toward her gesticulating wildly and seeming only now to notice her. Mara backed away from this bedraggled revenant in alarm.

And then she realised who he was.

Or once had been.

For this was the Englishman she had seen knocked unconscious in the courtyard and dragged away. Mara gasped, for he appeared so drastically changed. His skin had taken on a grave-like pallor and his wild eyes bulged from their sockets, either in fight or in fright she could not ascertain. What had they done to him? How could he have become so far removed from the cocksure man who had inflicted such flirtatious looks upon her at luncheon?

He kept glancing about as though speaking to others, though only he and she stood in the passageway for all else was either cold emptiness or impenetrable shadow. He shuffled nearer toward her still, his red-rimmed eyes blazing madly. Then, before she had time to react, he cried out in a high-pitched voice that would have been comical if it were not so murderous in its intent. It reminded her of the terrible chanting of the throng in her village when they had put the mansion and its inhabitants to the torch. Mara backed away, intent on fleeing, but the crazed Englishman was upon her in seconds. She gagged as he clamped his fat hands around her throat.

The candle fell from her hand.

Her head began to thunder with the sound of her own pulse as he began squeezing the life out of her. She tried to fight back, but her efforts were in vain. She was unable to move against the ferocious onslaught of his shock attack. Hideously, she could see the sweat of his exertions trickling from his hairline and across his pasty skin. All went silent, and she prepared to let darkness take her.

CHAPTER TWENTY-EIGHT

The chill presence of phantoms haunted Grayson's every tortured step, a cold fog of fear tightening every breath in his throat, as he toiled his way up the narrow, spiral staircase.

He heard their fingernails scratching against stone as they crawled after him, could smell the charnel decay of their rotting flesh, and inside his head, he heard their whispers.

The war dead were part of him somehow, insinuating their way into his heart and into his mind and bringing with them some fathomless guilt that he had hitherto held at bay.

The whispers spoke in overlapping voices of his betrayal and of their abandonment. With each hissed syllable their rallying cry became evident to him. Each of these phantoms, or echoes from beyond the grave, or whatever unholy thing they were, had been left to die on his watch.

Their whisperings combined into a deafening, accusatory whirlwind between his ears that made it impossible for him to separate one howling complaint from the whole. Reaching, at last, the top of the stairwell, he clung onto the sides of his head with his hands and screamed at the voices to stop.

And they did.

The ensuing silence was an enormous relief, and mad tears poured from Grayson's eyes. *There, there. Stiff upper lip, old chap,* he told himself. And yet, his tears flowed on.

His blood ran cold when he heard a whisper – singular this time, and yet with the force of a battalion – in his ear.

"A tear for each one of us ..."

At the dread sound of the whisper, Grayson felt an onslaught of fresh panic seizing his very blood like a disease. Fear once more took hold of his entire person. He looked madly about for the source of that disturbing whisper, seeking it out but at the same time terrified at discovering its source.

He turned.

Row upon nightmarish row of rotting soldiers stood in the passageway before him, their combined ranks in the hundreds. They stood as if to attention in the drill yard, the eyes of the ones who still possessed them horribly yellow-white. Some, their amputation stumps writhing with maggots, leaned upon the walls for support. Others carried one another, in death as they had in life, their bony arms slung over shoulders that looked too fragile to bear any weight at all. This was the very frontline of death and he cowered at its vanguard.

Yellow teeth gleamed sickly beneath dull eye sockets. Head wounds issued forth noxious fluids. Chest cavities torn open by shrapnel gave visceral insight into their fleshly workings. Each of these walking dead regarded him with a look so lifeless that it made his knees tremble beneath such a gaze. The troops just stood there, some swaying atop their bent and battered legs, as though waiting for a signal from their field commander.

He stammered at them to retreat, pleading madly with them to leave him be. All the while he attempted to retreat himself, but his fear-frozen limbs denied him any such recourse. He looked on aghast as the battalion of wraiths began to shuffle toward him. It was as though his terror-stricken voice was their clarion call. Their dead bodies pressed in upon him, an unstoppable wave of death. One of the soldiers whispered to him, his foul graveyard stench making Grayson sick to his stomach.

"Coward ... You deserted us ... Left us for dead ..."

Screaming in terror, Grayson reached out and clamped his fingers around the soldier's throat in a futile attempt to defend himself.

CHAPTER TWENTY-NINE

Mara blinked her eyes open and saw the horrifying face of the Englishman before her. His bloodshot eyes bulged red as he tightened his iron grip around her throat. She tried to plead for mercy, but felt her last breath choking within her windpipe.

Her legs gave way beneath her as she swooned.

Then, all of a sudden, the horrible tightness at her throat ceased.

Grayson's eyes were the size of ripe plums, just a lash-length from her own, and looked as though they might pop out of his skull. His mouth fell open and she smelled the taint of stale liquor, heady on his breath. He looked down and Mara thought of a child who had dropped his plaything.

She looked down, too, and saw a rosy stain bloom across the Englishman's shirt, its source the three vicious metal spikes that now protruded from his stomach.

Mara looked into his red eyes once more and found only confusion there. He made a hideous belching, squealing noise and then dropped to the floor, dead.

And then, free of his clutches, Mara screamed. For, behind the Englishman stood his killer. The stranger's open robes revealed that every inch of his sweat-slicked skin was covered in weird tattoos. His eyes blazed in dark triumph. This man did not look like a saviour to Mara. In fact, he looked intent on murdering her next.

With her back to the wall, she had nowhere to run. Terror-stricken, she saw him raise his pitchfork, ready to finish her. His face was a mask of brute intent, and those eyes spoke only of darkness. She saw the same betrayal in those eyes that she had felt as a child, and wondered if their lives had somehow always led them to this point. To this passageway, in this castle. Fates intertwined, with one the victor, the other the victim, and yet neither able to escape the dark passengers of their guilt. The dread words from the note seared into her mind. *You ... I know what you have done. Tonight, a reckoning is at hand.* Defenceless, Mara leaned against the wall for support. The tattooed man bared his teeth. His knuckles were pale from gripping the handle of the pitchfork so tightly. He meant to deal another killing blow.

Before it came, a vast shadow fell cross the both of them. Something had blotted out the torchlight from the passageway beyond. A massive axe sliced across Mara's line of vision and she saw the tattooed stranger's head separate from his body then tumble, hair over exposed neck, across the flat of the enormous axe blade before rolling to the floor. Mara heard a sickening squelch as the head hit stone. The tattooed torso stood, arterial blood arcing in a fountain from the neck wound, before it too slumped to the floor revealing the monstrous man standing behind it.

It was the American.

Mara tried to scream, and then tried to move, and failed at both.

She watched in abject terror as the giant American took a handkerchief and mopped at his brow as casually as if he were merely chopping firewood. Then, he stooped, leaning on his axe as though it were a walking stick, and began rifling through the tattooed man's pockets. His eyes lit up with elation as he retrieved a brown leather book. He flicked through it, seemingly oblivious to Mara's presence. Apparently satisfied with his find, he tucked the book away into his own pocket.

Then, crouching to the floor, he grabbed hold of the man's severed head by its blood-soaked hair and lifted it with him as he stood.

He looked straight at her, and Mara clamped a hand over her mouth to stifle a moan of terror. He looked utterly terrifying, standing at full height with the tattooed man's severed head dangling from one massive hand, the enormous axe in his other.

Numb with fear, Mara tried to tell herself that she did not mind, so long as he made it quick. She felt her blood freeze and her bowels churn as she watched him lift the enormous axe into the air. This was it. All of her earthly struggles leading her to die here, in a castle far, far away from home. Mara winced as the axe rose higher. Cold tears fell from her eyes as the American loomed closer.

He leaned into her until his nose touched hers and then snarled a single word.

"Run."

CHAPTER THIRTY

Mara ran.

The castle's damp air burned cold in her throat and froze the tears in her eyes. She ran in a blind panic, not caring about her direction of travel so long as it was away from the brutal American.

Why had he spared her, and only her? He had not hesitated to behead the tattooed man. If the Englishman had not already lain dead at her feet, she imagined the American would have wasted no time at all despatching him with similar remorselessness. So why her? Those blue eyes of his revealed nothing of compassion about his character, so his mercy could not have been borne of anything approaching pity. Ever since she had become aware of him aboard the train, she had witnessed only a coolly calculating quality to his behaviour. Even as she ran, her heart pounding in her breast, she had the nagging feeling that she was simply another pawn in whatever dark and twisted game he was playing. Mara disliked feeling this way. He had told her to run and she was doing exactly that. Even so, she had to admit that she had no other choice right now.

The air grew cooler, and the flaming torches in their wall brackets fewer, as she ran on. Eventually, she encountered the deep well of a staircase she did not recall having seen before and so elected to descend it. Chills ran through her as she navigated the steps in the erratic light of the flickering torches. Out of breath from her flight, Mara trod the last few steps of the staircase and found herself in a low-ceilinged passageway that led to an arched opening some yards ahead. Catching her breath, Mara glanced over her shoulder and saw the staircase empty behind her. Good. She had not been followed. Steeling herself against the unknown, she walked toward the opening, treading softly all the while. Here, the passageway opened up into a large chamber of some kind. It had a vaulted ceiling, supported by thick stone pillars, and was lit only by a collection of half-melted candles. Some of the candles stood atop circular wooden tables, and others dripped on the ledge beneath a single arched window made impassable by a lattice of iron bars. A random collection of wooden chests and overturned chairs gave the impression that this cellar had been ransacked, but as Mara approached the centre of the room she saw that the chests were in fact wooden coffins.

She grabbed one of the candles from the nearest ledge and prised it away from the stone, spilling hot wax down the front of her clothing as she did so. Holding her hand behind the candle to reduce its glare, she held it aloft to see if there was another way out of this charnel place. The candlelight exaggerated the shadows of the coffins, causing them to loom large upon the walls, their ominous shapes becoming harbingers of death. Her eyes searched the shadows for an exit. There. A series of steps led up to a raised dais on the far side of the room and beyond it she could just see the steep incline of further steps inside an alcove.

Hoping she had found her way out of this awful, musty place, Mara began to walk toward the dais leading to the alcove. Hearing a scuffling sound, she wheeled round in alarm. Her candle revealed the quick movement of a rat, scurrying out from beneath one of the coffins. She had probably disturbed the rat by invading its territory – but now she was altogether disturbed by it.

Giving the spot where she had seen the rodent a wide berth, she brushed against another of the coffins. Her heart skipped a beat when she heard another sound, this time a low scraping. Mara tried to ignore how the noise had seemed to come from within the coffin itself. She backed away from it slowly, gripping the candle tight in her fist – and saw the lid of the coffin slide open before falling with a deafening clatter to the floor. A hand emerged, impossibly white, and crawled over the side of the coffin like some monstrously pale arachnid. The woman who clambered out was clad entirely in white, her black hair streaked with grey. She stood before Mara, dead but alive, and with a terrifying hunger in her eyes to equal that of the rat Mara had, only moments ago, disturbed.

Mara backed away, terrified, and heard movement from behind her. She turned sharply and saw another coffin lid open, revealing another cadaverous woman. She ran toward the dais. Another coffin lid burst open and out crawled a third. The trio of white-clad revenants looked to one another with expressions of quiet amusement. They looked young, their features frozen in time, and yet each had the countenance of a statue. It was as if something ancient and eternal dwelled behind their unblinking eyes.

"Look, my sisters," said the first, "a playmate has come to join us."

The second licked her lips, and said nothing. She didn't have to.

The third smiled thinly at Mara before purring, "Join us, Mara. We shall know such frolics together, in the night. You can play with us forever and ever."

Mara felt a pang of terror upon hearing the strange woman speak her name. How could she possess the clairvoyance to know such a thing? Mara shook her head dumbly and continued backing away, hoping she would be able to outrun them and reach the stair.

A look from the first woman betrayed their true intent. She had glanced into the shadows opposite the alcove. Mara risked turning her back on the women to see what lurked there, and saw the top-hatted stranger from the train. As he stepped into the circumference of her candlelight, his features were revealed to her – or rather, the distinct lack of them, for he no longer had his collar up around his face. His skin was deathly pale, just like that of the unholy trinity of women who had stolen from out of the coffins. His eyes were grey in colour, matching his lips, which he repeatedly licked as he stared at her revealing the tips of sharply protruding canines. He looked as nondescript as the next man. He could easily be a bank teller, or an insurance clerk, or one of the ticket collectors aboard the Carpathian Express. And yet, there was a fierce intellect somewhere behind that bland visage. His eyes spoke only of his intent to murder her where she stood, unless she acted.

On instinct, Mara's fingers moved to her throat, and she realised that was what he was staring at. He licked his lips again and those sharp, overlong teeth gleamed in the light from her candle. She felt the links of the necklace chain beneath her fingertips, warm to the touch from the heat of her fear. Looping the chain around her fingers, she pulled the crucifix from beneath her clothing. The stranger's eyes widened, the pupils narrowing to black pinpricks. He raised his hands to his face as though protecting himself from the sight of the cross, the shadow of which fell across his face as Mara held the candle directly behind it. The man stumbled backwards and tripped on a piece of upturned furniture. Fiercely aware that she was still vulnerable to the trio of women, Mara then turned the crucifix toward them. They hissed like wildcats and recoiled, no sooner had they seen it. Heart in her mouth, Mara sidled up to and then across the dais until she reached the alcove. Still holding the cross up to the room and all of its dread inhabitants, Mara located the first step with the toe of her boot. Then she took a deep breath before she turned and ran up the stairs as fast as the incline would allow.

Within moments, she heard footsteps following her.

Mara drew on whatever courage she had left in her, summoning her last vestiges of survival instinct to help her reach the top of the stairs. Whatever primal force dwelled within her, and had kept her alive all these years against the odds, propelled her on. Even so, doubt crept into the periphery of her psyche. She found herself hoping that she would not find a locked door at the summit, trapping her inside the stairwell with the revenants at her heels. The thought of those pale hands reaching for her in the dark was almost too much to bear, let alone the savage bites from those sharp and hungry teeth. Mara glimpsed faint light now at the top of the stairwell and this bolstered her resolve. Where there was light, there was hope. Groaning at the painful extent of her exertions up the steep stone steps, she willed herself onward. Almost at the top, she stumbled forward and broke her fall painfully with her free hand. A jolt of pain shot up her wrist, reminding her that she was still alive. She could still feel pain. Not like those walking cadavers that pursued her even now. The women moaned – a terrible litany that spoke only of deathly intent. The awful, mournful sound provided the final impetus for Mara. She reached the final stair, at last clambering over it and then stumbling onto the flat surface of an antechamber floor.

Before her loomed the interior aspect of a massive, dark tower. Huge steps swept majestically up to a set of double doors, studded with iron and bearing the insignia of a coiled dragon.

And, before those doors, stood the American.

CHAPTER THIRTY-ONE

The American stood facing the tower doors with his back to Mara, the dead stranger's severed head dripping blood onto the stone steps at his feet.

Hearing the terrifying hisses of the revenants pursuing her up the stairs, she shut the stairwell door behind her and latched it. She knew it would not take four bloodthirsty devils long to break it down. Shuddering at the prospect, she turned her attention back to the American on the tower steps. He had told her to run, and she had inadvertently caught up with him. Perhaps he had meant for her to meet her death in that charnel vault? And if she made herself known to him now, would he once again show mercy? She could not fathom the inner workings of a mind as devious as his.

Watching from the shadows, she saw the American begin to ascend the steps. Just then, Mara heard a terror-inducing *scritch-scratching* at the door behind her. Her heart leapt into her mouth as she saw the latch slowly rising. Leaping to her feet, she quickly engaged the door catch to stop it from opening. As the hideous clawing and scratching sounds gave way to frantic bangs and growls, Mara wondered how long the door would maintain its barrier between her and the creatures trying to break through.

Glancing back at the American, she saw him hurl the severed head onto the top step. It landed and rolled to a halt against the doors with a sickeningly wet thud.

And then, with a deafening click, the huge doors swung open.

Mara watched the American step over the threshold. The doors opened wider, apparently of their own volition, revealing a vertiginous and winding stair. The huge man proceeded up the steps and disappeared from view.

Hearing the snarls and gnashing teeth of the vampires from behind the door, Mara proceeded in the direction of the only exit that lay open to her.

Up the tower stairs.

Reaching the top stair, she heard the low rumble of the American's voice. A plan began to formulate in Mara's mind. She took a deep breath.

The tower room felt enormous after the confines of the spiral stair. The room was a single, enormous square, with a flaming torch at each of its corners. A single, tall window afforded a view of the night sky beyond its open shutters. The tower was situated so high above the world outside that the trees and mountains seemed like distant memories to Mara. A full Blood Moon hung like a threat over the landscape, casting its sanguinary glow across the floor of the room, which was furnished in an opulence beyond that of Baron Meinster's mansion house from her childhood. Yet, whereas the baron's mansion had been a distasteful extravagance vulnerable to the wrathful flames of the villagers, this place felt like a fortress floating high above a kingdom that quaked in its shadow.

Everywhere Mara looked she saw rich spoils of gold and crystal, twinkling tantalisingly from chandelier to footstool. A suit of armour, heavy and black, stood sentry-like in a corner. The room felt hot and humid, and to her right, Mara saw a fire roaring within a hearth hewn from the castle's thick outer wall. The skilled hands of artisans had sculpted the fireplace into the detailed relief of a dragon's head. Flames danced behind fearsome, chiselled fangs the size of Mara's arm. Furs and rugs lay strewn over the stone floor and furnishings, and dark drapes cast their velvet shroud around the room. The overall effect was one of walking into the tent of some invading warlord at the epicentre of his campaign. An entire culture existed in this singular space. Its trappings told a tale of violent warfare, ceaseless pillage, and the omniscient ego at its vanguard.

At the centre of this sanctum sanctorum stood the American, the dais beneath his feet decorated with a circular, occult design. As Mara's eyes adjusted to the light of the torches, and the crimson cast of the moon, she discerned a pentagram – symbol of unholy black magic – bordered with strange glyphs and other symbols. She took great care to remain unseen in the shadows of the huge doorway.

"I have played your game and now I come to claim my reward," the American said. "Proof lies severed at the foot of your steps. I choose the sword as my prize."

The American had his back to her, but his companion was facing Mara and, as their eyes met, she saw an instant flash of recognition in his rodent-like gaze.

"Are you certain you wish to claim the sword? It bears a heavy price."

"I have made my choice."

"Very well. To the victor, the spoils, but answer me one question: why did you choose to spare the girl? She is all that stands between you and your escape."

Mara gasped as Klove looked straight at her. The American did not even look at Mara, but seemed to know of whom Klove had spoken.

"Spare me your lies. We both know that there is no such escape. I will tell all, but I demand an audience with your master."

Klove nodded and shuffled aside, and Mara saw for the first time a sword and shield mounted upon the wall behind him. The shield bore the same dragon crest she had seen above the tower doors, inlaid in ruby red and gold. The sword's huge blade seemed to be ablaze, a trick of the torchlight upon its polished surface. A single ruby was set into the gold hilt, as large as a wolf's eye, and glowing angrily red. Striding past Klove – a mere fly to be swatted away – the American stepped up to the sword. He stood before the weapon for one awestruck moment, and then reached forward to pluck it from its wall mounts.

Mara heard the timbers of the crypt door smash open, below. She knew the vampires would be upon her any moment and readied her crucifix, but felt her resolve begin to falter. Mara was unsure that the cross would repel the undead without its bearer having the true Christian faith to wield it. An image seared into her mind: the first tarot card that she had ever pulled from the deck she had inherited from her mother. It had been The Blasted Tower. Its meaning was mutable, she knew that now. Either she would meet her end standing before the dark tower, or she would find some way to conquer her fears and survive. She closed her eyes and focused on that mental image. All her life Mara had called on higher powers to guide her hand as she turned the cards. She hoped now that those powers might be aligned with those signified by the cross she held in her trembling hand.

Opening her eyes she saw the damned crossing the threshold into the tower room, their eyes red with bloodlust and their teeth gleaming yellow-white.

"Back, foul things!" Mara exclaimed, holding the crucifix aloft.

With snarls and hisses, the top-hatted stranger and the trio of female revenants recoiled from the crucifix.

Her plan was working!

Mara backed away slowly in the direction of the dais, holding the cross out like a warrior's shield. She then lowered the crucifix to allow the revenants to follow her. When she reached the foot of the dais, she quickly turned and retreated. Wary of the cross, the vampires closed in on their new prey.

The American turned to face this new threat.

But instead of attacking, the vampires threw themselves to their knees in front of Klove.

"Let us take him, Master," they pleaded, their voices thin with hunger. "Are we to have nothing tonight? Let us feed on him. We have brought you the girl."

The American's brilliant blue eyes widened in utter shock. He wheeled around and glared at Klove.

"You?" he said, "You are the master?"

A cruel look of glee oiled across Klove's face.

"Finish him," he said.

Mara saw sudden movement as Klove reached for the sword and snatched it from its plinth. How had the old butler moved so fast? He held the sword in his hand for a moment and then hurled it into the air.

And into the hands of the vampiric stranger.

Baring his fangs, the stranger hissed, snakelike, as he caught the sword. His eyes seemed to turn black with hatred. As he wielded the sword, his entire physicality seemed to change from one moment to the next. It looked to Mara as though the sword was now wielding *him*, weaponising him to do its bidding. His bones cracked. Muscles and sinew twisted and ripped. Even his teeth seemed to grow sharper, longer. He held the sword aloft, the gaze from his dark eyes falling like ruin upon Ernst Von Sammler.

Mara crept away into the shadows at the corner of the room. The American had been usurped! He took a step back. Even a brute as fearsome as him would falter before the cutting edge of such a sword – and the sharp-fanged *strigoi* who held it within his grasp. Mara saw the American register the danger he was in and she followed his gaze. On one side stood three undead brides of darkness, creeping toward him like a promise and a threat. On the other, their unholy offspring: the stranger and his terrifying sword.

Mara saw the American take a sharp breath. He raised his axe as if to strike … and then tossed it aside, reaching instead into the folds of his greatcoat with a speed that contradicted his bulk. In a heartbeat, he had unstoppered the vial he now held in his hand. And in another, he flung its contents into the bland death mask that was the stranger's face.

The stranger screamed, an obscene, shrieking howl that made Mara clamp her hands over her ears. She watched as he recoiled, the flesh of his face burning and then melting away. He dropped the sword and fell to his knees, his hands gripping onto his ruined features. When at last Mara saw the revenant's screaming skull through tangled flaps of smouldering flesh, she shut her eyes. And then, hearing a sickening thud, she opened them again.

The American had caught hold of the sword as it fell and then swiftly used it to behead the stranger. She looked on in horror as the stranger's severed head rolled to a halt and then caught fire – the flesh burning away in a fury of black smoke until only the skull remained. Mara gagged at the sight of the hollow eye sockets and protruding fangs.

A chorus of hideous whining sounds emanated from the trio of vampire women, children mourning their dead pet. Mara knew that was exactly what the stranger had become to these vile brides. One of them stooped and lifted the still-smouldering skull of the stranger they had sired and then prepared to turn her fury upon his murderer.

The American roared with bloodlust, the triumphant sound echoing around the tower room as though heralding its new master. Then, he appeared to look right through Mara, who felt her knees weaken to see that his eyes had blackened just as the stranger's had, moments ago. A dark wave of hideous power seemed to emanate from the American and Mara felt a shard of terror strike her heart.

The vampiric brides were upon him in a frenzy of teeth and claws, mouths open wide to reveal their lethal fangs. With a single swing of the blade, the American beheaded two of them. The last of the women cast aside the stranger's skull. With a wail as loud and as angry as a banshee's, she hurled her body through the air at the American, her fury boundless. She meant to avenge her fallen sisters and their undead plaything.

At the moment of impact, the American simply tilted his blade upwards, impaling the woman though her chest. Her banshee wail faltered, replaced by a pitiful sputtering sound. Mara felt a pang of sadness at the look of utter defeat on the woman's face. She coughed up thick blood, so dark as to be almost black, a damned thing dying upon a cursed blade.

The American lifted the sword higher, until it was almost vertical over his head, and the revenant's body slid further down the sword until it met the hilt, where it slumped, lifeless. He tossed her aside as though she were a ragdoll.

Mara watched with disbelieving eyes as the women's flesh simmered and cooked, falling from their bones and into dust – until only their skeletons remained beneath the shrouds of their tattered bridal gowns.

The American had seemed to grow in stature for every moment he had wielded the sword. His greatcoat could barely contain his broad shoulders. Pure evil seemed to pump through his veins. His footfalls pealed like thunder as he circled the room in triumph, swinging the sword through the air as though contemplating who to murder next. To Mara's horror, his eyes were now as black as coal.

"Now you die, little man," the American spat at Klove. "You are finished, *Master*."

The American strode toward the servant and then thrust the sword's blade directly at his heart!

Mara blinked. The American's sword had thrust into an empty space where, just a fraction of a second ago, Klove stood vulnerable to the attack.

The manservant had disappeared.

The American whirled round, slashing with the sword into yet more thin air. His blackened eyes widened in dumbfounded surprise.

Then, impossibly, Mara saw a hand burst through the American's chest. Pale bony fingers, with nails so long and sharp that they resembled talons, grasped the American's still-beating heart. Those hideous fingers closed around the beating heart like a spider clutching its prey and crushed the organ until hot blood spat from each of its chambers. Then, the hand shot back, pulling the heart with it and ripping it from his body. The American teetered for a moment, dumbly holding onto the cursed sword. Mara saw with horror that he had a fist-sized hole in his chest where his heart used to be.

"A pity, really," Klove said, his voice sounding musical, and younger somehow.

The American toppled from the dais and fell, lifeless, to the floor. His eyes had returned to their bright blue colour, and were fixed in the glassy gaze of an anguished death.

The man holding the American's heart in his hand looked like Klove, but appeared to be changing before Mara's very eyes. His features lengthened, somehow. His posture straightened, and all the colour in his skin ebbed away until he was as pale as moon dust. He crushed the American's heart in his fist until it was nothing but pulp, which he tossed onto the dead body at his feet. Then, quick as a fly, he licked the blood from the tips of his fingers, staining his thin lips crimson. He smoothed back his hair, revealing a sharp widow's peak. As his fingers slid through his tresses, they grew into flowing black locks.

Thunder crashed outside, and Mara winced at a sudden flash of lightning. From deep within the bowels of the castle came a frightening rumbling sound, as though its very foundations had been broken.

The man who was no longer Klove regarded Mara's terrified awe with a look of amusement as he climbed down from the dais. Then, in the merest instant, he stood right beside her! Mara shuddered. She hadn't been aware of him walking to her at all, and yet now there he stood. How could anyone – or anything – move with such silent speed? It was as though he held dominion over all of time and space.

Mara staggered backwards, suddenly aware of the dead bodies littering the floor at her feet. And yet, she still lived. But for how long before this monster tore out her heart and crushed it while she looked on, powerless to defend herself?

"I am Count Dracula, and this is my house," he said, revealing the long, sharp canines of a vampire. "And you, dear Mara, are the victor in my game tonight."

How did he know her name?

"Oh, I can see into your soul, child," he said, matter-of-factly, as though reading her thoughts, "and it is almost as darkly corrupt as my own. The dark seed of your guilt germinates within you."

He took her hand into his, and her mind imploded with a spike of darkness at their sudden, yet immutable psychic connection.

You ... I know what you have done ... I know what you left behind ... in the forests of the place you once called home.

His voice was inside her head, her thoughts his, and yet still somehow her own.

Darkness travels with you, Mara, and ever shall. Until your entire being becomes consumed by it. And then, you shall know only the night, and the sweet music of all its fell creatures.

Count Dracula's voice resounded inside her skull like a dark lullaby. She felt at once entranced and repulsed by it, seduced yet appalled. As his velvet tones echoed into silence, she returned to the present, and the intimate gloom of the tower room. She watched the count lick the blood from his lips and felt gripped by the desire to give him her own, to offer it freely. Her fingers reached idly for her throat, finding the fabric of her dress and tugging at it, exposing the flesh of her neck! Her fingertips brushed against the delicate ridge of a vein that pulsed with life within. And then, she remembered the silver crucifix in her hand.

Dracula recoiled from the cross as she held it before him, its afterimage reflected in his dark, brilliant eyes. He hissed – the same feral, animalistic response as the revenants from the vault. Whether she had passed or failed some final test, she did not know. The spell was broken, and Mara felt not only release from her reverie but also bereft at having lost the primal, psychic connection with a force beyond her understanding. She was a mere mortal, and he was something ... *other.*

Mara blinked away hot tears she had not known were there. The booming noises continued from deep within the castle, becoming ever louder. An ear-splitting crash erupted from the fireplace, which exploded in a burst of flame as the thick castle wall split from floor to ceiling. Masonry began to crash down, coating the drapes with the thick, grey dust of ages as it fell. The entire room seemed to tilt from the impact of some monstrous, subterranean force, knocking the black suit of armour from its plinth. The armour clattered to the floor in a heap of metal before falling stones of lethal size buried it from view.

"This way!" Count Dracula commanded, leading Mara over to one of the red velvet drapes behind the dais.

Beside it in the shadows, unseen by Mara until now, stood a tall coffin. The casket had been fashioned from the finest, polished black wood. Its clasps were of the finest gold, as was the crest of a dragon that adorned the lid of the coffin.

Beneath the crest was a single letter – "D".

The count reached out with one taloned hand and pulled aside the drape, revealing an arched doorway that gave access to a narrow, winding stair.

"Go," he instructed, "follow the stairs all the way down to their end. You will find your way from there."

Mara opened her mouth to speak, but he cut her off with his urgency.

"Go now, child!"

In the tower room behind them yet more masonry fell, revealing the inner structure of the building. The very fabric of the entire castle was caving in upon itself. Roof timbers were exposed to the night, unearthed like skeletons in excavated graves. Cold starlight penetrated the room as the last of the tower's roof tiles fell. The shattered crystal of the once perfect chandeliers lay strewn on the floor, now mere debris. All around her was dust, flame, and ruin.

"Come with me! The castle is falling!" Mara pleaded through the chaos.

For all the terror the count had instilled in her, he had saved her from the American's demon blade, had made her the victor in his battle royale. She could not just let him perish here, alone. She reached for him, open arms imploring.

The count merely smiled, and then began to laugh hysterically, the cacophony of the castle's destruction subsuming the discordant music of his voice.

As the tower fell away in a maelstrom of destruction, fractured stone, shattered wood, and exploding glass trailed through the air – and tumbled with finality into the ensuing void.

Mara leapt back onto the landing leading to the secret stair. Coughing, she waved a cloud of dust away from her blinking eyes. As the dust settled, Mara saw that Count Dracula had disappeared, along with the edifice of his dark tower. Through the open wound of the ruptured wall, Mara saw the first glimmers of daybreak flickering to life where the Carpathian mountaintops met the sky.

As the castle walls imploded around her, Mara began her frantic, final descent.

CHAPTER THIRTY-TWO

The very walls of the narrow staircase seemed to vibrate around Mara as she rushed down the steps.

Her heart pounded in her ears, loud enough almost to drown out even the deep rumbles and crashes of the collapsing castle. The entire staircase shook, and Mara was thrown to one side. She reached out and steadied herself against the wall before continuing her desperate descent. Dust and mortar rained down from above. An all-pervading fear of being buried alive seized hold of Mara. Agonising moments passed before her feet delivered her safely to the bottom of the stairs.

"You will find your way from there," Count Dracula had told her.

Before her hung another tapestry. At a glance, anyone venturing down this stairwell might be forgiven for thinking they had met a dead end. But Mara knew different. Or at least, she hoped she did. She reached out and pulled back the tapestry as though it was a curtain. The thick fabric was heavy with dust and she held her hand over her nose and mouth to avoid inhaling any more unwelcome detritus.

An open doorway behind the tapestry led her through and into a narrow passageway, lit by candles. She removed one from its wax-coated candelabra and pushed on, following the passageway as it took a sharp left turn. At the end of the passageway stood a single door. Mara dashed to it and pulled it open. A rush of cold air ruffled her hair and made her candle flicker. She quickly cupped her hand around the flame to prevent it from sputtering out. Stepping through the door, she found herself on the landing of an expansive spiral staircase several times the size of the count's secret stairwell from his now ruined tower.

Mara steeled herself, for she could not see the bottom of the staircase in the dark. The parts she could see wound so deep she imagined the staircase must burrow into the very mountainside that was the castle's foundation. She took a tentative step from the landing and onto the first step. In an instant, the sounds of destruction seemed far away, the walls around her thick and seemingly impervious to the castle's collapse. The candle flickered alarmingly as the door behind her slammed shut with a frightening bang. Mara glanced back and saw there was no handle on the inside.

The only way out was down the great spiral staircase.

CHAPTER THIRTY-THREE

The sheer stone stairwell was treacherous, and becoming narrower with each turn.

The scant light from the single candle made each footfall a leap of faith. Mara's blood- and dust-coated skin carried with it a sour, metallic odour that overpowered all her other senses in the cloying dark.

Then, a cool breeze taunted her from somewhere deeper, promising a way out, but one that felt utterly beyond her reach. Her forearms prickled with gooseflesh as the cold air wafted over them. She almost lost her footing on the next uneven step and her free hand brushed against the curved stone surface of the wall. It was cold to the touch, and slick with a layer of slime. The further she descended, the more it felt as though those hideous, slimy walls were closing in, over and around her.

Swallowing her whole.

She gasped.

The tightening of fear at her throat made each breath more desperate than the last. The stairwell narrowed further still, accentuating her panic as she stumbled from step to step. Mara lost her footing and hot wax spilled from the candle, burning her hand. Only the nub of the candle remained. It sputtered and she glimpsed a phantasmagoria of shadows on the walls and ceiling. The acrid smell of burning hairs on the back of her hand mingled with the salt tang of blood from her wounds.

In the flickering orange light of the candle, she glimpsed the shape of a writhing girl tied to a stake. Her fevered brain conjured sounds of the crowd, chanting and mocking. The scent of burning hair worsened. Bile rose to her throat at the sickening aftertaste of burning flesh. Mara heard the girl's screams inside her skull as the image distorted, enveloping the stairwell in a nightmare conflagration of pain and death. The heat lapped at her tender flesh hungrily. Just as it had Carmella's.

Burn the witch! Burn her!

Her mind became a fog of fear as her memories took shape around her. The vengeful mob, wielding fire. Brothers turning against brothers, mothers against sons. Entire families put to the flame. Her village, a smouldering ruin where once she had played as a child. Yet, in spite of the devastation, Mara had never looked back. They had killed her father. Let them turn on each other, eat one another alive, for all she cared.

Mara battled on down the stairs. Still no sign of a way out. The candle sputtered once more, and then died, plunging her into darkness. Mara felt it closing around her in a black embrace. She tried to scream, but no sound would come. She reached out her foot, trying to reach the next step, but found only thin air. She fell, expecting her fragile body to break upon hard, unyielding stone. On and on she fell, tumbling into an endless, formless abyss. Freezing air blasted into her lungs.

This time her scream came, echoing all around her, full throttle, as she plummeted along with it—

—and hit solid ground.

Winded, she tried to catch her breath. All was dark, and dank, around her. A wave of despair washed over her. A broken doll, sitting in a pool of her own lifeblood, she would surely lie forgotten in that dark stairwell until madness and death took her.

Blinking the tears away from her eyes, she saw something penetrating the dark. It was a thin crack of light! If only she could find the will to move her legs, she could crawl toward it. In that moment, Mara put all her past nightmares behind her. She was on her own, as she had been ever since she had left her village. Her isolation had not made her weak, it had sharpened her resolve, had helped her to survive rather than submit to the will of others.

She crawled toward the light. As she drew nearer, she saw that it described the outline of a door. A way out! Mara gritted her teeth through the pain in her legs and hands, and stood up. Limping painfully, she knew she was just feet away from the exit.

She reached for it through the darkness and, finding the door, she pushed it open with the last of her might—

EPILOGUE

M ara sat bolt upright and blinked the dark remnants of her nightmare away.

What an altogether horrid dream!

Reaching for the handrail beside her bed in the sleeper carriage, she steadied herself against the movement of the train. She used her free hand to disentangle her legs from her sheets, which were in some disarray. The small of her back felt cold, and she realised with shame that her nightdress was drenched with perspiration. She stood and walked over to the wall-mounted gas lamp. It flickered, conjuring unwelcome memories of the candle and the crumbling stair from her disturbing dream. She reached up to the little brass wheel and dispelled her night terrors with a turn of the valve. Her cabin now fully illuminated, Mara crossed to the nightstand and poured water from a jug into a goblet. Her throat was dry and she did not cease drinking until she had drained the vessel. Composure returning with each passing second, she placed a hand to her breast and willed her heart to settle into something of a regular rhythm. Soon enough, her breathing returned to normal. The fire and blood of her nightmares had receded, leaving her to the order of the day.

Tucking a loose strand of hair behind her ear, she turned to survey the eveningwear she had hung on the rail above her valise. She took the jug and poured the remainder of the water into the enamel bowl set into an alcove in the wall. Above it, a mirror revealed her reflection. The leading was beginning to show around the edges of the looking glass, casting a vignette around her reflected face. This only served to increase her focus. The hazel eyes looking back at her looked sharper now that she had fully emerged from her slumber, but her nightmares had left their dark, half-moon shadows beneath them. She gazed instead upon her olive skin, which had lost none of its lustre despite her travels. She blinked, her lashes like petals reaching for sunlight, coming back to life. Arching her spine (as a cat might, in readiness for the hunt), she licked her lips and felt hunger stirring in her belly. Taking a silk scarf from the back of the chair beside the sink, she tied back her hair and set about readying herself for breakfast.

POSTSCRIPT

C ount Dracula stood in the safety and the solace of the shadows of his dark tower and surveyed the wild, untamed beauty of his Carpathian kingdom that lay beyond his balcony. The first rays of the accursed sun bled red across charcoal clouds that mottled the sky, heralding daybreak. His sharp ears detected the sound of a whistle some miles away. The count's all-seeing eyes witnessed the first wisps of smoke from the locomotive rising above the tips of the mountains beyond the treeline.

He recounted the previous night's revels, mulling over every tiny detail of play and counterplay as though they were morsels to savour. As it so often did, the night had brought with it such succulent delights. He looked down at the moat and chuckled in remembrance of the Russian's untimely demise. And could it really be true that the collector had begun to remember after all this time? An intriguing development that even he had not foreseen. In life, Von Sammler's crimes had been truly monstrous. The man exhibited a bloodlust to rival even his own, making it all the more surprising that the lost girl had won out. He began to contemplate which role he would choose to play tonight and how the wheel might turn this time.

The last stars of nightfall had begun to retreat from view, and so he retreated to his chamber. He had work to do. Turning his back on the fiery sky with a swish of his cloak, he crossed to his desk and sat down. He placed a fresh sheet of parchment upon his blotter and then, taking up his pen, began to inscribe the first of tonight's letters.

You ... he wrote, *I know what you have done. Tonight, a reckoning is at hand* ...

THE END?

ABOUT THE AUTHOR

Frazer Lee is the Bram Stoker Award® nominated author of seven novels.

Winner of the Edgar Allan Poe Gothic Filmmaker Award, Frazer's screenwriting and directing credits include the acclaimed horror films *Panic Button* and *The Stay*.

Frazer is Reader in Creative Writing at Brunel University London, and resides with his family in Buckinghamshire, just across the cemetery from the real-life *Hammer House of Horror*.

Crisps are his downfall, talk him down from the ledge at: www.frazerlee.com

ARE YOU BRAVE ENOUGH
TO PLAY
DAMNATION: THE GOTHIC GAME?

Can you survive the night?

Damnation: The Gothic Game is a battle royale-themed horror board game for 2–8 players, where the last surviving player is declared the winner. Players control one of a cast of unique Victorian-era scoundrels as they take turns to explore the deadly rooms of Count Dracula's ancient castle in search of powerful cards to help them survive the night.

Find out more, if you dare:
www.blacklettergames.com

Printed in Great Britain
by Amazon

10775856R00137